# CATCH

DEBORAH BLADON

FIRST ORIGINAL EDITION, OCTOBER 2020

Copyright © 2020 by Deborah Bladon

All rights reserved. No parts of this book may be reproduced in any form or by any means without written consent from the author.

This is a work of fiction. Names, characters, places and incidents either are the product of the author's imagination or are used fictitiously. Any resemblance to actual persons, living or dead, events, or locales are entirely coincidental.

ISBN: 9798681385035:
eBook ISBN: 9781926440606

*Book & cover design by Wolf & Eagle Media*

https://deborahbladon.com

# CHAPTER ONE

*MAREN*

"DUDLEY'S DADDY can't keep it in his pants." I flick a wrist toward my laptop screen. "I have another five DMs from women this morning."

"You have even more responses to your post on the Manhattan Lost and Found Dog group?" My roommate, Arietta Voss, comes marching into the dining room to get a better look.

I glance up and take in her outfit for the day. For a twenty-two-year-old petite blonde with gray eyes, Arietta looks nothing like you would expect her to.

The hem of the frumpy navy blue skirt wrapped around her waist hits her legs mid-calf. It's not half as bad as the lime green blouse she's buttoned up to her neck.

"You must still be beating the men off with a stick, Arietta."

She lets out a laugh. "I am trying to be professional, Maren."

"You're never going to get that sexy beast of a boss of yours in bed if you keep dressing like that."

Her eyes widen behind her dark-colored, rectangular eyeglasses. "Dominick Calvetti is still in Italy, and besides, I would never sleep with someone I hate."

"You hate him as much as I hate my vibrator," I quip.

With a shake of her head, she crosses our apartment to pull a bottle of orange juice from the fridge.

Technically, it's my apartment. If we're getting down to actual specifics, it belongs to my father. He bought this three thousand foot dream on the twentieth floor of a high rise in Tribeca as a gift for me.

It's not a standard gift, though. There are terms, and I'm already in violation of one of them.

I lost my job yesterday.

I need to stay gainfully employed to keep this lavish roof over my head.

Keeping it over Arietta's head is important to me too. We met at a vintage jewelry store a year ago. Arietta mentioned that she was looking for a place to live, and even though she's six years younger than I am, I invited her to move in.

We're as close as sisters now.

After pouring herself a glass of juice, she bends down to stroke her hand over Dudley's head. "How are you today, sweetheart?"

Arietta has been calling him that since I found him wandering the street last night without a collar.

A whole host of responses to my posting on the Manhattan Lost and Found Dog group have clued me into his name.

They also directed me toward his irresponsible owner.

Keats Morgan.

Mr. Morgan is a twenty-nine-year-old sports agent. His

client list is impressive, but that's not why he's so popular in this city.

Every reply to my posting about the lost dog has come from a woman.

Twenty-three women have messaged me to say that they met Dudley when they spent the night with Keats.

I push my curly red hair back behind my ears. "I sent Keats a DM on Instagram, but so far, he hasn't responded. When I called his office just now, the woman who answered the phone put me on hold and then hung up on me."

"I'd get fired if I tried that trick." Arietta bites her bottom lip. "I'm sorry. That was insensitive. I can ask at work if there are any available positions."

Arietta works as an assistant at a wealth management firm. My background is in public relations. "You're an angel, Arietta, but I'm going to put out some feelers today."

I'll do that very quietly, so my dad doesn't get wind of my employment status.

"If you know the address to Mr. Morgan's office, I can drop the dog off on my way to work," Arietta offers.

Keats Morgan is all kinds of gorgeous, and I haven't been on a date in two months. I could use a glimpse of something tall, green-eyed, and handsome today.

"I'll get dressed and head over to his office." I point at the cute black and tan Yorkshire Terrier sitting on the floor watching us. "Say your goodbyes to Dudley because he's about to be reunited with the man who can't keep him on a leash."

---

"WHAT THE EVER-LOVING-FIG bar are you doing with Dudley?"

"Huh?" I question the way-too-good-looking man in front of me.

His black hair looks like it was once perfectly styled, but a wayward lock has curled onto his forehead. His green eyes pierce into me as he crosses his arms over his broad chest.

If gold medals were awarded for sexy forearms, Keats Morgan would be world champion. I should thank him for taking the time to roll up his shirtsleeves today.

This man is the definition of hot-as-hell, but what did he just say to me?

"Are you listening to me, Mary?" He pokes a finger in the air toward me. "Why the hell do you have Dudley? Goddammit, I swore. Shit. I did it again."

I shake my head because that is a lot to absorb.

"My name is Maren," I repeat for the second time.

I introduced myself when I got off the elevator, marched toward his office, and found the door ajar. The desk outside was vacant, so his receptionist or assistant, or whoever should be fielding his calls and visitors, is MIA.

"Forgive me for that, Maren." He flashes a dimpled grin before he lets out a sneeze.

His bicep flexes beneath the thin fabric of his blue and white striped button-down shirt as he raises his hand to cover his nose.

"Bless you," I mutter.

His right brow arches. "I'm too far gone for that."

Shaking my head, I push Dudley toward him because my hand is now dripping with puppy saliva. He's an affectionate little dog, but I don't do animal kisses.

Keats sneezes again, backing up as he does. "Get him the hell away from me. Heck. I meant heck."

Glancing around, I feel like I've stepped into an alternate

universe where the hottest guy in the world crossed paths with a charming nerd, and Keats Morgan was created.

"Mr. Morgan." A woman with long brown hair dressed in a tailored white suit glides into his office. "I'm back from my break."

The woman stares a path through me when she catches sight of me out of the corner of her eye.

"I'm Maren," I say to her even though I doubt she cares. "I'm here to return Mr. Morgan's dog."

Maybe this woman will take Dudley off my hands so I can get the hell out of here.

"He's not my dog." Keats looks directly at the woman in the white suit. "You were supposed to take care of this, Jamie."

"I did." She approaches him. "I took care of it."

"Then why the hell is he with her?" His arm waves in my direction.

"You said hell," she points out.

"What?" he barks.

Dudley does too.

I try to calm the dog with a kiss on the head.

"You swore." Jamie sighs. "You know what that means, sir?"

"You're fired."

My gasp gets lost in the sound of Jamie's almost scream. "What, sir?"

"You are fired," Keats repeats.

"Because I pointed out that you swore?" Jamie tosses her hair behind her shoulders. "You told me to do that."

"I entrusted you with Dudley." He steps toward me but then takes two measured steps back. "You told me you'd take excellent care of him, and she found him on the street."

Jamie looks at me. "Where did you find him, Mary?"

"Her name is Maren." Keats shoots me a glance before he turns his attention back to Jamie. "Why the fuck does it matter where she found him?"

"Sir, again you…"

"Swore," Keats interrupts her. "I sure as hell did, and I will again if I goddamn feel like it. You gave me your word that you'd take care of my sister's dog until she gets back to Manhattan. You failed, so you're fired."

Jamie stomps a shoe against the marble floor. "I am going to take this up with Human Resources."

"Do I look like I give a fuck?" Keats pushes on the rolled-up sleeve of his shirt. "I want you out of here now."

"I'll go." She glances at me. "This is all your fault."

I stalk toward her with Dudley in my arms. "How so?"

"You should have just let him be." Her finger trails in the air in front of Dudley's face. "He's a lot of work. He barks too much, and he squirmed out of his collar when he was with the dog walker. I couldn't deal with it, so I gave him to my sister. Dudley must have slipped out of his collar again when she took him for a walk."

"Get the hell out," Keats orders. "You have two minutes to vacate the building before I call security."

"Fine." Jamie turns on her heels. "I hated working for you anyway. You can tell the poor soul that you hire to replace me that I wish them luck. You're a monster."

## CHAPTER TWO

***Keats***

AS SOON AS Jamie slams the door, I turn to the woman holding Dudley in her arms.

Maren, the dog rescuer, is beautiful.

Her curly red hair reaches halfway down her back. That paired with her ocean blue eyes and long legs makes me feel things.

I'd say I'm getting weak in the knees, but the reaction my body is having to her hits higher than that.

"I apologize that you had to witness that." I shove a hand in the front pocket of my navy blue pants. "I should have spoken to Jamie in private."

"No harm, no foul." Maren shrugs. "I do need to go."

She approaches me. For every step forward she takes, I retreat by a larger step.

"I'm trying to give you the dog."

I stare at her. "I can't take the dog."

The toe of her black-heeled sandal taps against the floor.

This woman might not have dressed to impress anyone today, but *fuck me*, she's hot in her boyfriend jeans and white button-down shirt that's tied in a knot at her waist.

The sound of a phone buzzing lures her gaze to the black bag slung over her shoulder.

She adjusts Dudley in her arms before she fishes in the bag and yanks out a phone.

I watch her lips move as she reads the message on the screen.

*Can you come in for an interview today?*

The spy camp my folks sent my brother and me to during summer breaks when we were kids has paid off. The instructors taught us how to crack codes and dust for fingerprints. It was my roommate at the camp who showed me how to pick a lock. He also schooled me in the art of reading lips.

That's a skill that comes in handy when you negotiate for a living.

Maren looks up from her phone. "I have an appointment, so you're going to have to take Dudley whether you like it or not."

"I'm allergic," I say honestly. "That dog and I are not compatible."

"I'm sorry to hear that, but it's not my problem."

I can't argue with that, so I take another approach. "My sister dropped him on my doorstep when she went on vacation. She told me that Yorkies are hypoallergenic and I'd be fine, but Dudley didn't get that memo."

"There must be someone here I can give him to." She glances over her shoulder. Two people pass by the open door of my office.

I've already tried to convince every single one of my employees to adopt Dudley temporarily. No one was willing to sign up even with the promise of a vacation in the tropics or a bonus added to their paycheck.

Jamie was my last resort.

Dudley licks Maren's hand, so I make my first offer. "I'll pay you to take care of him for me."

Her blue eyes widen beneath long lashes. "You'll what?"

"I need someone to watch him for the next six weeks," I say.

That's a give or take because my sister, Sinclair, is somewhere in Europe. She's been gone for three months, and before that, she took off for two months to Australia. Eventually, she'll land back in New York and take possession of her dog. *I hope.*

"I can't take care of him." She brushes the idea away with a terse chuckle. "I have to be somewhere, so just take him from me."

"Why can't you take care of him?"

I know it's a ludicrous question. This woman doesn't know me. She sure as hell doesn't look all that comfortable getting licked by Big Dud, but I need her help, and I don't want her to leave. I like her.

I don't know why the fuck I like her, but I do.

"I have a job interview, Mr. Morgan." My name comes out like a dirty word from her lips. "I have to go home and get ready for that."

"I'm offering you a job," I point out. "I'll pay well."

"I work in public relations." She shifts Dudley to her other arm. "I'm not taking on a job as a dog sitter."

I get it. She thinks it's beneath her. I've been there. I bagged groceries during my teenage years. I hated every fucking second of it. The truth is that job taught me that if you work hard, you'll be rewarded. I missed it when I quit after high school.

"Are you open to taking on a job as my assistant?" I scrub my hand over my forehead. "I need a new one."

"Since you just fired yours," she says in a whisper.

"You'll start at seventy five a year and perks."

That lures her eyebrows up. "Seventy five thousand dollars?"

Nodding, I rest my hip against my desk. "You'll have a car and driver at your disposal, and you'll receive a monthly expense account for incidentals. Jamie used hers for manis and pedis, and whatever the fuck an astrologer does."

Maren's eyes narrow. "How many assistants have you had in the past year?"

*Well, shit. We're going there?*

"Several." If I keep it general, maybe she won't press.

"How many?"

*Jesus.*

"Not counting Jamie, that would be three," I say as casually as I can.

Her gaze drops to her phone when it chimes again.

This time she doesn't move her lips when she reads whatever popped up on the screen.

"My interview is in two hours." Her voice rises. "I need to go now."

"Whatever they are offering you, I'll double it."

*Why the fuck did I just say that?*

Dudley whines as she slides him from one arm to the other again.

Maren bites the corner of her bottom lip, and my cock thanks her for that by coming to life.

I shift so she doesn't get a glimpse of the tent I'm popping in my pants.

"You're going to double what I'm being offered by the company I have an interview with?" She shakes her head.

"You're serious? You don't even know if I'm qualified for Jamie's position."

"Can you answer phones, write emails, and arrange for Dud to get to doggy daycare every day?"

"He goes to doggy daycare?" She plants a kiss on his head, and I'm jealous of the little shit.

"Five days a week." I push a hand through my hair. "I had a nanny for him the rest of the time, but she quit. And then the guy I hired after her…"

"Quit?" she interrupts.

"They didn't like living with me." I shrug. "They had an entire floor to themselves. I have no idea what the problem was."

She rakes me from head-to-toe as if she's silently surveying the problem.

"A lot of people quit when they work for you." She glances at Dudley. "What's going to happen to him when he's not at doggy daycare?"

"I'll give you an extra five thousand if you take him home with you every night and if you watch him on the weekends."

Her chin lifts. "Make it ten. Add that to my yearly salary of double your original offer, and you have yourself a deal, Mr. Morgan."

I hold in a smile. "It's Keats."

"Jamie called you Mr. Morgan."

"You're not her," I point out.

"When do I start?" She glances back at the people walking past my office. "Do I need to sign anything?"

"You'll start taking care of Dudley immediately." I round my desk. "I'll call Human Resources to put together an employment contract for you. Give me your full name, number, and address so we can take care of that today."

"I'm Maren Weber," she starts before she rattles off a number with a 917 area code and an address in Tribeca.

Maren Weber is already living large if she calls that building home.

"I'll be in touch," I say, meaning that I want to touch her, but small steps win the race.

"Can I get Dudley's things?" She asks with a slight smile. "He must have favorite toys and a bed. Does he eat a certain brand of food? Last night, my neighbor gave me some of the food she buys for her dog, but I'm sure Dudley would prefer whatever he eats regularly. I want him to feel at home at my place."

Dudley thanks her for asking by licking her cheek.

"I'll have it sent to your apartment."

She nods. "I'll take off for now. Thanks for the job, Keats."

The surge of desire that races through me stops my heart from beating for a half-second. "You're welcome, Maren. Welcome to Morgan Sports Management. I think you'll like it here."

Her non-response tells me she's not convinced of that, but I'll make sure she has the time of her life while she works for me.

# CHAPTER THREE

***Maren***

IF I COULD BOTTLE the look on Arietta's face and sell it, I'd be richer than my parents.

It's pure joy with a touch of surprise.

In celebration of my landing the best job I've ever had, I ordered dinner in tonight.

Arietta is a big fan of anything French, so I called up my favorite French restaurant, Sérénité, and had them whip up a feast fit for the best roommate in the city.

It set me back a few hundred dollars, but it's worth every penny.

Dudley is dining well tonight too. After a delivery person dropped off several boxes containing Dud's belongings, I rummaged through them. The dog food he's been living on is subpar, so I called my cousin Donovan Hunt. He's a vet and the knower of all things animal related. He recommended a grain free brand. One of the vet assistants who work at his clinic stopped by with a complimentary bag for Dudley to sample.

When I filled his dish with it, he barked his approval before he devoured it all.

Arietta's gaze darts from the food on the dining room table to Dudley wagging his tail.

Maybe her excitement is more about the dog and less about the coq au vin and chocolate soufflé.

"What's happening?" she asks quietly. "Why is the little sweetheart here, and is that our dinner?"

I divide and conquer the questions as I reach for the worn-out leather bag in her hand. "We're going to take care of Dudley temporarily."

She willingly hands over her purse before she bends down to scoop him into her arms. He greets her with a plethora of kisses to the chin.

"I had dinner delivered tonight," I say nonchalantly as I drop her purse on the white leather couch that neither of us finds the least bit comfortable.

My father bought this apartment furnished. Nothing in here has any personality other than Arietta and me. I can add Dudley to that list now.

"We're having French food for dinner?" The question is punctuated with the rise of her brows. "Is it someone's birthday?"

"Yes." I nod with a sheepish grin plastered on my face. "Every day is someone's birthday."

That lures a laugh from her. "I'm lost, Maren."

I reach to take Dudley from her. "Get into something less grandmotherly, and we'll eat before the food gets cold."

Her gaze skims her outfit. "You're not the first person to tell me that I look like a grandma today."

I'm not surprised. "I had a bottle of wine delivered too."

She claps her hands together. "I'll put on a sweater and yoga pants. I'll be back before you can count to ten."

---

"I NEEDED THIS." Arietta sips from the wine glass in her hand. "This is so good."

In the time it's taken her to finish half a glass, I've polished off two. I need to slow it down if I'm going to get through explaining everything that happened today before I drift into a coma of inebriation.

"It hit the spot," I say, nodding my head. "We're celebrating something."

Her eyes scan my face. Arietta has a natural instinct when it comes to reading people. Since we started living together, I've learned that it's useless to try and hide my emotions from her.

"I'm all for celebrating the fact that Dudley is staying with us." She reaches down to scratch under his chin.

He's been sitting on the floor next to her chair since we started dinner. So far, he hasn't been rewarded with anything other than the frequent touch of Arietta's hand as she pets him. French food scraps are not on the menu for him tonight.

"It's only until his owner gets back to town," I point out because I don't want Arietta getting too attached to the dog.

She tilts her head. "Keats Morgan is out of town?"

"He's in town." I look at the bottle of red wine but decide not to refill my glass. "His sister owns Dudley. Keats has allergies, so he needs someone to watch the dog at night and on the weekends. Dudley goes to doggy daycare during the day."

"Doggy daycare is a thing?" She smiles.

"It's a thing, and tomorrow I'll drop him off there."

She lets out a breath. "Why are you taking care of him? I feel like I'm missing something."

I've been hesitant to share the news about my new job because I'm not even sure how I ended up with it. I was lining up an interview while I was in Keats's office. It was for the position of a sales rep for a company that specializes in selling flavored seltzer water.

I politely declined that after Keats fired Jamie and looked to me as her replacement.

"When I went to drop Dudley off this morning, Keats offered me a job," I confess.

"I think taking a job dog sitting is admirable, Maren." She perches her glass in the air as if she's about to toast me. "Keats Morgan chose the right candidate for the position."

"I'm not so sure about that," I say apprehensively.

"What do you mean?"

"He hired me to take care of Dudley, but there's more." I reach for the bottle of wine and pour no more than one mouthful in my glass.

Arietta watches my every move. "Tell me."

I spread my arms out at my sides as if I'm putting myself on display. "You are looking at Keats Morgan's newest assistant."

Her entire face lights up. "He gave you a job?"

I nod.

As quickly as the smile appeared, a frown takes its place on her lips. "Why don't you look happy about it?"

"I'm happy," I reassure her. "There is one red flag that I kind of looked over before I agreed to take the job."

She pushes her glasses up the bridge of her nose. "What kind of red flag are we talking about?"

"I'm his fifth assistant this year."

"Fifth?" She questions. "He's gone through four assistants in one year?"

Scratching my chin, I realize just how bad that sounds. "He fired the last one right in front of me."

Reaching across the table, Arietta pours what's left of the wine in the bottle into my glass. "Drink up, Maren. Your new boss sounds worse than mine."

# CHAPTER FOUR

*MAREN*

DROPPING Dudley off at doggy daycare was harder than I thought it would be.

It wasn't because I got all teary-eyed at the prospect of not seeing him again until tonight. One of the caregivers at the center decided that I should be welcomed into her world with a hug, followed by a quick trip down her memory lane of pets.

I sat next to her with Dudley in my lap as she scrolled through hundreds of pictures of two Dalmatians that she had saved on her phone.

After twenty minutes, I finally told her that I had to meet with my new boss. She scurried away with Dudley tucked under her arm. Her promise that he'd enjoy himself wasn't necessary.

I could tell he was happy to be there based on how hard he was wagging his little tail.

I take a breath as I ride the elevator up to the floor that houses Morgan Sports Management.

I'm not officially an employee yet.

A delivery person dropped off the contract this morning, just as Arietta was leaving for work. She asked if I was ready to sign it, but I told her that I needed to talk to Keats first.

I have questions that I want answers to before I agree to be his executive assistant.

Skimming my hand over the skirt of the simple black dress I'm wearing, I try to shake off the anxiety I'm feeling. It's been sitting on my shoulders since my dad tried to call me an hour ago.

I won't lie to either of my parents. I'm their only child, and even though they've used their wealth to open doors for me, they expect me to be a thoughtful, compassionate, and honest person.

Telling them that I landed this job will make them both happy, but I need to be sure that I'm not making a mistake before I do that. I hope that talking to Keats will help put my fears to rest.

This isn't my dream job, but if I accept it, I'd like to keep it longer than the last four people who worked as Keats Morgan's assistant.

---

I STEP off the elevator and into the middle of what I can only call a *team meeting*.

Keats is standing on the desk that's right outside his office door. If that's my future desk, I'm going to use a portion of my monthly expense budget to buy disinfecting wipes to clean the entire surface. The shoes on his feet are expensive, but I have no idea where the hell they've been.

I glance to my left and then the right. People have gathered around. I can't spot one without a wide grin on their face as Keats addresses them.

"Remember what I always say." He drops his hands to his hips. "Quitters never do anything worth talking about, so don't be a goddamn quitter."

The room erupts in laughter.

Several voices all call out the same thing in unison. "You swore."

Keats raises a hand in the air. "I know. I owe a hundred to the fund."

"A hundred times eight." A female voice rises above the noise. "We all heard it, so you owe for every single one of us."

"Eight hundred dollars?" Keats shakes his head. "Sh… shish kabob on a skewer."

I crack a smile when I hear laughter roll through the room again.

Keats smiles too, and it's glorious. The man is strikingly handsome with his hair slicked back into place today. He's wearing a charcoal three-piece suit with a white shirt and a gray silk tie.

The grin on his face widens when his eyes lock on mine as he scans the room.

As much as I try to erase the smile on my face, I can't. I toss him an awkward wave, and he reciprocates with a nod.

"I think I have a meeting," he announces to the crowd. "Get your asses back to work."

"That's another eight hundred bucks." A man's voice bellows over all the others trying to convey the same point.

"Nine hundred," Keats corrects him with his gaze still pinned to my face. "I owe an extra hundred. Maren heard it too."

Heads turn in the direction he's staring. I suck in a breath when eight pairs of eyes land on me.

"I'm Maren," I mutter as if it's not apparent.

"Clear the way people. I need Maren in my office right now," Keats says as he jumps from the desk. He nails the landing before he buttons his suit jacket. "With any luck, she'll be part of our team by the end of the hour."

With whispered hellos, the people gathered move aside to make room for me to walk to Keats's office.

I greet them as I pass by.

This office is a lot more laidback than the last place I worked. Staff meetings don't exist at Knott Public Relations.

I barely knew my colleagues even though I worked side-by-side with them for years.

"Welcome aboard, Maren." A woman passing by me smiles.

A man with graying hair perks both brows as he steps out of my way. "It's great to meet you. I'm Everett."

I nod. "It's nice to meet you too."

As I near the open door of Keats's office, I take one last look around. Maybe working here won't be so bad after all.

# CHAPTER FIVE

***Keats***

A MILLION QUESTIONS are swimming in Maren Weber's eyes. I saw it when she stepped off the elevator to find me standing on a desk talking to my employees.

I treat most of the people who work for me like family. We've cut our teeth together in this business. I opened shop with two employees seven years ago when I was fresh out of college with a dream and a small inheritance from my grandfather.

He was a sports fiend.

All he wanted was to meet his favorite baseball player, so I made it happen. In the process, I made some friends, and when it came time to sign my first client, I had my eye on a college ballplayer who had an older brother in the majors.

I was introduced to the younger brother by his sibling before the first game of the World Series. By the third inning, I had a verbal agreement in place to represent him.

That lit the fire beneath me. I've upped my game since then, adding employees and clients at a steady rate.

The only thing I haven't been able to master is hiring an assistant to replace the one who was by my side for the first six years I was in business. I'm hoping this time I got it right.

As Maren settles into one of the chairs in front of my desk, I drop into the leather chair I spend a good portion of my day in.

My office may not be the biggest in this city, but it has two things I need. I have a clear view of the Empire State Building from my window and a desk that once belonged to my grandfather. You can't beat that.

"You have questions," I say to Maren as she holds tight to the envelope containing the contract I had sent over to her apartment this morning.

She looks up. "I do, but I'm curious about something. It's about the swearing and the fund. What is that?"

"That's a long story."

It's not as long as it is fucked up. I'd rather not talk about it, but if she's going to take on the role of my executive assistant, she needs to know.

"I have a niece. She's eight." I glance at one of the framed pictures sitting on the windowsill. It's a recent image of my brother and his daughter. "I'm trying to set a good example for her, so I look to the people around me. They hold me accountable if I swear."

Maren nods. "So the fund is essentially a swear jar? Isn't a hundred dollars for each person who witnesses you swearing steep?"

"I donate the money once a month to a cancer charity in Boston."

That sets her back into the chair. Her shoulders slump.

She doesn't know what to say, so I fill in the blanks the same way I always do when anyone asks about the fund.

"My brother's wife died two years ago." I swallow hard. "I promised Stevie, my niece, that I'd do something to honor her mom's memory. It was Stevie's idea that I donate a hundred each time I swear."

"I'm sorry," Maren says quietly.

"I make a sizable donation every month regardless of how much I curse, but I am trying to curtail it to set a good example for Stevie." I take a breath. "My brother perfected the art of not swearing in her presence. I'll never live up to that ideal, but I'm doing what I can."

A soft smile settles on her lips. "I understand."

I don't. How does a thirty-two-year-old woman who has her entire life ahead of her die from breast cancer just days short of her daughter's sixth birthday?

*Life fucking sucks.*

"I expect you to call me out when I swear." I half-laugh. "My brother told me it takes fifteen days to break a habit."

"It's actually twenty-one days, and that's a myth."

"Fuck," I snap. "You're serious?"

"That's a hundred to the fund." Maren tips a finger in the air.

I smile. "If I told you that was a test, would you believe me?"

"No." She shakes her head. "I'm all about attention to detail, so I'll hold you accountable for the cursing."

"Damn right, you will."

"Damn is technically a swear, so that's two hundred."

I laugh. "You're good. You're maybe too good for this job."

The smile falls from her lips. "We should talk about that. I'm not sure I'm the right fit for this job, Keats."

"Why the he...heck not?" I question.

"You've had a lot of assistants in the past year alone," she points out. "I'm wary about that. I'm not perfect, so if you expect that, I'm not the person for this job."

Folding my hands together on the desk, I lean forward. "I don't expect you to be perfect, Maren. I expect you to be honest, loyal, and do the job to the best of your ability."

Her gaze drops to her lap.

I push on because I want this woman to work for me. That unexplainable pull I feel for her is there again, and it's stronger than it was yesterday.

"I fired Jamie because she lost Dud, but there's more to that story." I exhale sharply. "She was on her tenth or eleventh warning before she volunteered to take over caring for Dudley."

That draws Maren's chin up, so she's looking at me. "That's a lot of warnings."

"Jamie pushed the boundaries from day one." I exhale, still frustrated with my former assistant. "She'd waltz into the office an hour late. She'd forget to give me messages. She's called in sick three times this month."

"She wasn't sick?"

"I'd say no based on the fact that she used that time to go on shopping sprees." I laugh under my breath. "She'd post non-stop on Instagram, tagging her fellow employees to show them what she was buying."

"Wow." Maren smiles. "That's bold."

"That's one word for it." I squint. "After I called her out on that and told her that her time here was done, she promised to clean up her act. She offered to take Dudley home to care for him. I thought we had turned a corner."

"Then she lost him," Maren says.

"And she took a forty-five minute break after showing up

for work thirty minutes late yesterday." Chuckling, I shake my head. "She gave me hell when I fired her, but it was time for her to go."

# CHAPTER SIX

*MAREN*

"THREE HUNDRED," I say quietly. "You said hell."

Keats laughs. "I have to think before I open my mouth around you. If I don't, I'm going to end up broke."

The anxiety I felt when I stepped off the elevator is slipping away, but it's still lingering.

"Every other person I've fired was for just cause," Keats says as though he's reading my mind. "They all left with a severance package that was more than fair."

I don't expect him to go into details. I'm surprised he was so candid about Jamie's dismissal.

I don't see this job as the end game of my career, but I want it to last at least until I can find something suitable in public relations.

"Can I ask you a question, Maren?"

I glance across the desk at him. "Sure."

"How the heck did you wind up here with Dudley yesterday?"

I point at the phone in my hand. "After I found him, I snapped a picture and posted it on a Facebook group for lost dogs in Manhattan."

Leaning back in his chair, he narrows his eyes. "Who responded?"

*Who didn't?*

I fight the urge to say that because I'm not a saint either. I'm going to work for the man, not be in charge of his social calendar. Who he sleeps with isn't my business.

I choose my next words carefully. "The post was shared more than fifty times. I received messages from a few of your friends."

"A few of my friends?" he repeats my words with a furrowed brow. "Like who?"

Does he expect me to rattle off the names of all the women who responded to my posting about Dudley?

I pat my hand against my thigh. "I can't recall their names, but I'm glad they got in touch. I was worried that since Dudley wasn't wearing a collar, I wouldn't find his owner."

"Sinclair would have given me supreme shit if I lost her dog."

"That's another hundred," I tell him before I ask for clarification. "Sinclair is your sister?"

Tilting his head, he smiles. "Another hundred added to the fund, and yes, Sinclair is my globe-trotting sister."

That begs the question of whether he has another sister, but his family situation has no bearing on my job, so I skip past that and mention mine. "My cousin is a vet. I dropped in to visit him at work one day. I had to wait to see him because he was implanting a microchip into a dog."

"What the hell is that?"

"That's five hundred total since I sat down." I smile. "The

chip contains all the owner's information so that any animal shelter or vet can use a special reader to access that information if a lost pet is brought in."

"Holy...he...helpful device," Keats stutters out. "Dud needs one of those."

"I can arrange for that," I offer before I realize the words have left my mouth. "If you want, that is. Or if your sister is alright with it."

"Sinclair will love it," he says matter-of-factly. "I'd appreciate it if you set that up."

Nodding, I make a note in my phone to call Donovan. "I'll get in touch with my cousin and move forward with it."

"Are you ready to move forward with the job?"

My head darts up until my eyes lock on Keats's face. "I think so."

"Once you sign the contract, you'll officially be my assistant." He points at the envelope in my lap. "Can you start on Monday?"

Since today is Friday that gives me the weekend to ready myself for what I'm sure will be the most interesting job I've ever had.

"I'll start on Monday."

"Let's head over to Everett's office." Keats pushes back to stand. "He's the head of our HR department. He'll get you set up for payroll and everything else you need."

I need to know that I'm making the right decision, but I sense only time will tell me that.

As I glide to my feet, Keats moves to stand next to me. "I'm looking forward to working with you, Maren."

All I offer back is a smile because something tells me that being his assistant will have more twists and turns than a roller coaster ride.

# CHAPTER SEVEN

***Keats***

I SWING OPEN the door of my townhouse to find my favorite person in the world. Next to her is my brother.

"Stevie!" I hold out my arms, waiting for my niece to make the jump into them.

She doesn't let me down. She may be getting taller by the month, but our method of greeting one another hasn't changed since she learned how to walk.

I'm aware that there may well be a day that she won't want to hug me, so I take advantage of it now while it's still happening.

"How was Boston?" I look over her head at my brother, Berk.

"Fine." He rubs at the scruff that covers his jaw.

Fine means it was fucked up. I know his code words by now. He's taken on the role of sole parent to Stevie since his wife, Layna, passed away.

My older brother has always been my superhero. In the

time since he lost his wife, he's proven that he owns that title. I've never met a stronger man than him.

"Grandma and Grandpa were sad," Stevie clues me in with a sigh. "They were showing me a photo album. It had pictures of mom when she was in high school."

Layna's parents are still holding tightly to their grief. I'm not a dad, so I have no understanding of the kind of pain that comes with mourning a child, but I know loss. I loved Layna like a sister, and her death hit me as hard as a punch in the gut.

It knocked Berk flat on his ass for months, but he's moved forward. He took a leave of absence from his publishing company, Morgan Press, for half a year to focus on Stevie. Now, he splits his time between work and his daughter.

"Where is Duds?" Stevie cranes her neck to look around me.

I move aside to let them in before I close the door. "He's staying with my new assistant."

"Jamie has been your assistant for months, Keats." Berk points out as he slaps my shoulder. "Unless you fired her."

Stevie trains her blue eyes on me. "Did you, Keats?"

I've never carried the Uncle moniker with her. I've always been Keats. It suits me just fine.

Berk drags a hand through his dark brown hair. "Did you?"

It's not as though either of them held Jamie in the highest regard. They met her a couple of times when she stopped by here to have dinner with us.

"She lost Dudley," I state with a cross of my arms over my chest. "My new assistant found him and tracked me down."

"Thank goodness." Stevie twists her head, so her ponytail

bounces. "What is your new assistant's name and number? I want to set up visitation."

Berk huffs out a laugh as he rests a bicep against the wall. "You know that Sully gets riled up when she smells Dudley on you."

*Sully.*

I'm as allergic to that cat as I am to Dudley. Layna and Stevie cornered Berk five years ago when they brought home a kitten with an attitude. Since then, Sully has become part of their family. She's the reason that Dudley can't live with them. Sully won't make nice with dogs.

"I'll take a bath after I see him." Stevie shoves a hand into the back pocket of her pink pants. "I brought you something from Boston, Keats."

I know what it is, so I hold out my open palm. "I've been practicing."

"I'm still the champion," Stevie declares as she slaps a package of blue bubble gum into my hand. "You'll never beat me in the bubble-blowing race."

She's right, but I'll try again and again because I know she gets a kick out of it. Our tradition of her bringing me a package of this particular brand of gum started the day after her mom's funeral. I took Stevie to a convenience store a block from her grandparents' house after the service because Berk needed time. He had to tell Layna's parents that he wouldn't uproot his daughter's life and leave Manhattan behind.

I knew that the conversation would be an emotional one, so I took Stevie for a walk. By the time we got back with blue lips and tongues, the drama was over. Berk agreed to give Layna's parents all the access to their granddaughter they wanted.

Their weekly visits to Manhattan gradually shifted into

Berk making monthly trips to Boston with his daughter. They left Thursday night, so I'm surprised to see them back here less than forty-eight hours later.

"I thought I'd have an extra day to practice," I say, closing my fist around the package of gum. "It's Saturday. Weren't you scheduled to be back tomorrow?"

"It's my bestie's birthday tomorrow." Stevie bounces in her sneakers. "I'm going to surprise her in the morning with balloons and brunch."

"Kids your age know about brunch?" I question with a lift of my brow.

She gives me the once-over. "Men your age wear ripped jeans? Is that my dad's T-shirt?"

I glance down at the World's Greatest Dad shirt I'm wearing.

An ex gave me this shirt on April's Fool Day as a joke. I fell for it hook, line and sinker because I thought it was her way of telling me she was pregnant. She wasn't. I should have tossed the shirt out, but I kept it. Since today is laundry day, I dug through my closet to find whatever was clean.

I glance at Berk to explain the shirt to his daughter because I don't know what the hell to say.

"He's practicing for when he finally gets married and has a baby." Berk smiles. "Keats thinks he'll be the world's greatest dad."

Stevie lets out a full laugh. "No way. My dad is the best. You might be the second best, but who knows?"

I point toward the kitchen. "I ordered pasta from Calvetti's for dinner. It was delivered ten minutes ago. Lucky for you, there's enough for all of us."

"Spaghetti, here I come," Stevie yells as she takes off across the hardwood floors.

"You were expecting someone else, weren't you?" Berk

adjusts the collar of the black button-down shirt he's wearing. "Stevie wanted to stop by, but we can take off."

Since they only live three blocks from here, I'm used to their unannounced visits. I welcome them so much that I gave my brother a key to this place. He never uses it. He always rings the doorbell.

"It's just me for the night." I sigh.

"Are you recovering from last night?" he asks with a smirk.

"I ate a sandwich on the couch last night while I watched a full season of that teenage drama I'm not supposed to let Stevie watch."

Berk bites back a laugh. "You bastard. I knew you were the one letting her watch that."

"You swore," I point out, tapping him on his shoulder.

He ignores my comment. "Why did you order so much food, Keats?"

"Have you tasted the food at Calvetti's?" I arch a brow. "It's the best Italian food in the city. You try eating one serving."

I leave it at that. My brother doesn't need to know that I was going to cart the extra over to his place and put it in his fridge so he wouldn't have to think about what to feed his daughter once he got back from Boston.

"I want to hear more about your new assistant." Berk pats me on the back. "Dish up some food and give me all the details."

I follow behind as he makes his way to the kitchen. The only detail that matters is that I haven't stopped thinking about Maren since she left my office yesterday, and I'm counting the hours until I see her again.

# CHAPTER EIGHT

*MAREN*

I HAVEN'T HAD to face many first days on the job because I've only worked at a handful of places in my life.

My first job was at a fast-food restaurant on the Lower East Side. I worked there for two years while I was in high school. I went to a private school, and while most of my friends were partying hard on their parents' dime, I was earning money to go toward my college fund.

The deal I had with my parents was simple. If I contributed to my education, they'd support me by covering my tuition at the school of my choice.

I intended to go to Yale or Harvard, but my grades didn't get on board for that, so I went to NYU. I stayed at home instead of moving on campus. It was one of the best decisions of my life.

I interned at a recording studio during summer breaks in college. After I graduated, I worked at two different companies before I landed an entry-level job at Knott Public Relations. I worked my way up to Communications Specialist. My end goal was the position of Director of Communications.

Royce, my boss, took a leave of absence. He was the only person I reported to. When he left, his brother Christian stepped in to fill his shoes.

Christian may have co-owned the firm, but he rarely showed up to the office before Royce temporarily walked away.

We clashed almost immediately. I tried to respect the challenges Christian faced taking over control of the company, but when I noticed him making decisions that ultimately cost us clients, I spoke up.

I was fired with no notice, and a month's worth of pay.

Now, here I am a few days later with a job that pays me twice what I was making at Knott. According, to my employment contract, the position of assistant to Keats Morgan is straightforward. I'm overqualified, but that's not going to stop me from doing my best.

I'm counting on a stellar recommendation from Keats when I find another job in my field.

In the meantime, I'll bank the money I earn and learn what I can from the sports agent.

As I approach one of the guards in the lobby, I flash the badge that Everett, the Head of Human Resources, gave me last week. I'm early for my first day because I want to have time to organize my desk and get my bearings before my boss shows up at work.

The building that houses Morgan Sports Management is on one of the busiest streets in the city. I passed by the Empire State Building on my way here this morning. The first time I ever went there, I was with my dad. He took me up to the observation deck and told me that the city was mine to conquer.

I'm doing that by chasing my dreams. This job may be a temporary detour, but I need it.

The guard narrows his eyes as he looks over my badge. "Good morning, Miss Weber."

I smile at the brown-haired man. "Good morning to you."

I scan the front of his uniform for a nametag, but there isn't one, so I offer him a hand in greeting. "I'm Maren. I'll be working at Morgan Sports Management. You already know that from my badge."

He takes my hand in his. "I was given the heads-up by Mr. Morgan himself. Everyone calls me Ripley."

"Ripley," I repeat his name. "I'm early, but what better way to start a new job, right?"

"I've been here for five years, and I'm early for every one of my shifts." He smiles. "I'll get the elevator for you. I hope you have a memorable first day on the job."

---

AN HOUR LATER, my desk is organized exactly how I like it with the computer on the right and the office phone to my left.

I took a mini-tour of the office and found a break room equipped with two different coffee machines, a microwave, and a mini-fridge. I didn't bring lunch with me today because I plan on meeting up with Arietta to share a sandwich and an update on how my morning went.

That was her idea, and I quickly jumped on the chance to see a familiar face mid-day.

"How are you settling in?" Everett asks as he steps up to my desk.

I saw him exit the elevator ten minutes ago. He turned in the direction of his office, but tossed me a wave as he talked on his cell. From my limited time with him, I sense he's a good man who loves his family.

I counted three pictures of his wife and their two kids on his desk when I met with him last week.

"I think I'm settled." I laugh.

"That will change when Keats shows up." A chuckle escapes him. "He'll keep you on your toes."

Before I have a chance to quiz him further, the elevator doors slide open, and Keats appears.

Today, he's dressed in black pants, a white button-down shirt, and a gray suit jacket. The shirt is unbuttoned at the collar to give him a relaxed corporate look.

I glance down at the front of my blue dress. The last thing I want is for my boss to catch me staring at him.

"Good morning, good people," Keats says loudly as he walks past my desk. "It's a new week. That means it's a fresh chance to impress me."

The room erupts in laughter.

"I need to get to work." Everett slides a hand over his graying hair. "Good luck on your first day, Maren. If you need anything, you know where my office is."

Keats stops mid-step just as those words leave Everett's lips. "I'll give Maren whatever she needs."

I glance at my boss.

He perks a brow. "Join me in my office, Maren. I'll give you a quick rundown of what we're doing today."

I glide to my feet. Grabbing the tablet I found in the desk drawer, I suck in a deep breath. This is it. I'm about to find out what working for Keats is really like.

# CHAPTER NINE

***Keats***

*I'M FUCKED.*

I asked Ripley to shoot me a text when Maren arrived today. That was an hour ago. I was at home, debating what to wear.

That's right. I was going through everything that I picked up at the dry cleaner yesterday. I wanted to look good for my new assistant.

The last time that happened was never.

I finally settled on a pair of black pants that make my ass look fantastic. I know that as a fact because I've heard the comments behind me as I've made my way down the streets of Manhattan wearing these pants.

You can't go wrong with a white button-down shirt. I noticed Maren eyeing up my forearms the other day, so I'm getting rid of this gray jacket straightaway.

If she wants my muscular arms on display, I'll gladly give her that.

"Should I sit?"

Her question breaks me out of my lust fog.

I know I shouldn't want my assistant, but damn that blue shift dress she's wearing highlights her eyes and other parts of her.

I turn to face her. "Yes."

She drops into one of the chairs in front of my desk, so I do the same in my worn leather chair.

It's another inheritance piece from my grandfather.

One of her red nails swipes over the screen of the tablet in her hands. "What's on the agenda for today?"

Good question.

Every work thought I had was crowded out by my daydreams about Maren.

There's no way in hell that this is a good idea. I've never been attracted to anyone who works for me. That's not by design. My brain has naturally put up a barrier between work and play.

That's all fallen to the wayside because I'm feeling a rush of heat run through me as I watch Maren lick her bottom lip.

I drop my gaze to my desk.

*Think, Keats. Work. Think about goddamn work.*

"Pace Callahan."

Maren's gaze shifts from the tablet to my face. "What was that?"

"I have a meeting with Pace Callahan today," I say. "I want you there."

She scratches her right palm. "When is the meeting? Do I have time to research who Pace Callahan is?"

I hold back a smile. "You don't know who Pace Callahan is?"

Maren shakes her head, sending her red curls bouncing around her shoulders. "I don't."

"Fuck I wish he was here." I chuckle. "Pace won't believe someone exists who doesn't know who the hell he is."

"You owe two hundred to the fund." Maren shoots me a look. "I take it Pace is famous in some way?"

He was one of the most valuable baseball players in the major leagues until a shoulder injury cut his career short six months ago.

He's about to make waves as a commentator on a major sports network thanks to a two-year, eight-figure deal I negotiated for him.

"He used to be a good baseball player," I downplay his achievements. "We're meeting him to talk about his next steps."

"Was he kicked off his team?"

I can't tell if she's playing with me or not. "Something like that. I'll let Pace fill in the blanks for you."

"Fair enough." She shrugs. "What time are we meeting him?"

I glance at my watch. "We'll meet him for a coffee at ten."

Maren nods. "What do you need from me before then?"

Details. I want details about her life, starting with whether or not there's a man in it.

I opt for a more professional answer. "Jamie has a client list in a file on your computer. Take some time to look that over and acquaint yourself with the people we work with."

Pushing a lock of hair behind her ear, she smiles. "I can handle that."

I stand when she does. Watching her leave, I have to wonder whether I can handle working with her.

---

PACE CALLAHAN IS A THIRTY-TWO-YEAR-OLD, charismatic son-of-a-bitch who is flashing his pearly whites at Maren as we walk into the coffee shop that's a block from my office.

"Pace," I call out to him so he'll get his eyes off of my assistant.

It doesn't work.

"It's nice to meet you," he says to Maren in his best *I-want-you-in-my-bed* voice.

Maren stops mid-step and glances at me. "That's him?"

I don't know her well enough to read between the lines, so I can't tell if she's impressed that the brown-haired guy in the jeans and blue sweater is Pace, or if she finds him repulsive.

*Who the fuck am I kidding?* No one finds Pace repulsive.

"Has he considered a career as a model?"

"What the hell?" I mutter.

"That's a hundred to the fund, boss," Maren shoots back.

I swear that the smile on her face is meant to reassure me that Pace isn't her type, but that's swiftly pushed aside when she glides across the floor and right into his orbit.

"I'm Maren Weber," she announces as she drops her hand in his. "It's a pleasure to meet you, Mr. Callahan."

"It's Pace." He covers her hand with his. "You must be Keats's new assistant."

"I am." She tugs her hand free. "And you're his favorite client."

I'm about to call Maren on that because it's bullshit, but Pace buys into it. The wide grin on his face tells me he's eating it up. "I had an inkling I was."

"Let's sit and discuss your next chapter." Maren points at the café's counter and the barista waiting patiently for their next customer. "I'll get us each a latte. That works for you both, doesn't it?"

Her eagle eye spotted the label on the side of the empty cup atop the table Pace was sitting at. The word latte is bolded.

"That's my go-to." He smiles. "Keats made the right choice hiring you, Maren."

*I can't argue with that.*

My assistant is charming the hell out of my most aggravating client. Hiring her was the best move I've made in a long time.

# CHAPTER TEN

*MAREN*

"WE'RE CELEBRATING TONIGHT," Pace announces as I set the tray holding the lattes on the table. "Are you in, Maren?"

I glance at Keats as I take a seat between the two men. Since my boss is actively avoiding eye contact with me by staring at his phone's screen, I take that as a hint. Besides, I worked hard at my last job to keep my work friends separate from the people who will be there for me no matter what.

The two *work friends* I did have at Knott left for other positions months before I was fired, and neither kept in touch. It makes perfect sense since we never spoke outside of business hours.

"I have plans," I lie, although I'm considering rescheduling my lunch with Arietta to dinner as soon as I'm back at the office.

That draws Keats's gaze up. "You do?"

Maybe I misread his interest in his phone. If he needs me

to work tonight, I'll be there. I'm assuming that their idea of a celebration involves tequila shots and hooking up with random women, but I might be totally off base.

"We'll hit up a club," Pace says, ignoring the fact that I opted out. "I'll get a few of the guys together, Keats."

I breathe a sigh of relief because the last time I went to a club was six months ago with Arietta. We left without any men but with a bunch of memories of cheesy pickup lines.

"You're sure you don't want to come, Maren?" Keats questions.

I glance at him. "I'm busy, but thanks for the invite."

Keats bites the corner of his bottom lip. I can tell he's curious about my plans, but before he can push for more details, Pace clears his throat.

"The deal you secured for me is stellar, Keats." He bows his chin. "When I fucked up my shoulder, I thought baseball was in my rearview mirror."

I hear the gratitude in his tone.

"It'll never be behind you." Keats laughs as he picks up the cup in front of him. "Kill it as a commentator, Pace, and in two years, I'll secure you a deal that's even sweeter than the one you just signed."

Some people might mistake Keats's declaration as arrogant, but it's based in confidence.

I saw his client list. I don't know much about sports, but I did an online search of every athlete he represents and it's impressive.

"I know that you're taking your cut from the deal." Pace leans back in his chair. "But, if there's anything else I can do for you, tell me."

Keats pushes his cup to the side. "There's one thing I want."

"Name it," Pace blurts out without hesitation.

"Get me one-on-one time with Fletcher Newman."

A belly laugh escapes Pace. "You want to talk to the boy wonder? What the fuck makes you think I have any pull with him?"

I look to my boss to explain who Fletcher Newman is, but he's focused on Pace.

"In every interview the kid does, he brings you up." Keats taps his fingers on the table. "Have you not watched any of those?"

"I don't watch college ball games." Pace laughs. "I heard he was an up and comer from some of the guys on the team. That's all I know about Newman."

"In his eyes, you're the best pitcher in the history of the sport." Keats rests his elbows on the table. "I want face time with him, Pace. I need to represent him."

Pace sips from his cup. "So, what's the plan? What do you want me to do?"

Just as Keats is about to reply, my phone starts up on a ring in my purse. I meant to silence it during the walk here from the office, but it slipped my mind.

I was distracted after getting a glimpse of Keats's ass in the black pants he's wearing when he bent down to help a woman who had dropped her MetroCard on the sidewalk.

He might have the most perfect ass I've ever seen on a man.

Both men watch avidly as I reach in my bag for my phone. I see Arietta's name dancing across the screen. I know what she wants. She's looking to pin down a location for us to meet for lunch, but I'm going to suggest we go out for dinner instead.

"I need to take off." Pace pushes back from the table. "Come outside with me, Keats. Tell me what I need to do to get you a meeting with Fletcher."

Keats follows his lead and rises to his feet. "I'll see you outside when you're done, Maren?"

"I'll be there," I say with an over-exuberant nod. "I'll only be a minute."

"It was good to meet you." Pace flashes me a wicked smile. "I'm sure I'll see you soon."

"Until then," I toss back.

Swiping my hand over the phone to connect the call, I watch Pace and Keats exit the café. Damn, my boss looks just as good walking away as he does when he's on the approach.

He turns his head to glance over his shoulder, so I drop my gaze.

"Hey, Arietta," I say into the phone.

"If I'm interrupting something important, tell me," she whispers.

*I was just staring at my boss's ass.*

I keep that to myself. "I can talk for a couple of minutes. Can we do dinner instead of lunch?"

"That works for me. How is your first day so far?"

I glance out the café window to where Keats and Pace are standing. Keats grins when he catches my eye.

"So far so good," I say as my heart races.

"Maybe your future is with Keats Morgan, after all."

I laugh off her words. "I've worked with him for two hours. He's not my forever, Arietta."

"You don't know that," she lowers her voice. "Give it time, Maren. You might be exactly where you were always meant to be."

# CHAPTER ELEVEN

*Maren*

THE OFFICE IS EERILY quiet when I arrive for my second day of work. I stopped on my way to pick up a coffee, and by the example set forth by my generous father, Tim Weber, I bought a coffee for Ripley too.

I tagged along to work with my dad enough times to learn the value of treating everybody right. My dad owned an insurance company until he retired two years ago.

He was born with what he called a diamond-encrusted silver spoon in his mouth. My grandparents were filthy rich, and my great-grandfather was too. Inherited wealth can be as much a burden as it is a joy.

I step off the elevator exactly an hour before I start work for the day. Arietta needed to get to her office early to handle a call from her boss, who is still in Italy. We took Dudley to doggy daycare together before we made a pit stop to get our morning coffees.

I glance around the office. No one is in sight, but a sliver of light is peeking out from beneath Keats's door. I can hear the muffled sound of someone talking, or maybe it's more than one person.

I can't tell, so I take a few tentative steps closer to the door.

Keats's deep voice is unmistakable, and the generous pause every so often tells me that he's on the phone.

I glance at the office phone on my desk, but the light next to his direct line isn't flashing red, so he must be on his cell.

Setting my steaming hot cup of coffee on the desk, I drop my purse into the bottom drawer.

Just as I'm about to take a seat, a large bang startles me.

I stand straighter, my hands darting to my chest.

My heart races as I try and calm my breathing.

It does little good because another bang, even louder than the last, sets me back a step.

"Fuck this!"

I look toward Keats's office at the sound of his voice.

*What am I supposed to do? What if he's in trouble? Did he fall? Does he need help?*

"What the hell? Stop. Just stop."

The panic in Keats's voice is unmistakable, so I do what any good assistant would.

I grab the dusty umbrella hanging on a coatrack behind my desk, I march toward my boss's office door, and I swing it open.

My breath catches as I take in the sight in front of me.

Glitter rains down on my half-dressed boss as he turns toward me with his hands swatting the air.

My gaze travels from his unkempt hair to the shocked expression on his face. He's wearing a white button-down shirt, a bowtie, and a tuxedo jacket, but his legs and feet are bare.

On the floor in front of him is a glitter cannon.

As my eyes dart back to his glitter-covered thighs, he leans toward his desk. He grabs an empty bottle of champagne and positions it in front of his boxer briefs.

Shaking my head, I exhale once and then again. "What? Why? I mean…how?"

He drags his free hand through his hair. "Good morning, Maren. You missed a hell of a celebration last night."

---

ONCE I SAW that my half-dressed boss was fine, I took a seat at my desk.

Every part of me wanted to text Arietta so I could explain what I just saw, but I dropped my phone into the bottom drawer of my desk next to my purse.

I have to digest this before I can share it with anyone, because *what the actual fuck* is going on?

I steal a look at Keats as he comes strolling out of his office. At least he put on his pants, although he's still missing socks and shoes.

"I need you to arrange a trip for me, Maren," he says calmly.

I glance in his direction because are we just going to pretend that all the glitter in his office doesn't exist?

He lost the bowtie, and with his hair neater than it was, he looks shockingly gorgeous for someone who must have a raging hangover. The glitter specks on his face and in his hair force a smile to my lips.

"It's a trip for two," he continues. "Look into a two-week vacation in Fiji. I'm thinking of a five star resort with a private villa. The best food, massages, the works."

Envy tugs at me, but I shake it off because I'm not here

for anything but a job. It doesn't matter to me who he's heading to Fiji with.

Maybe it matters a little, so I push for more details. "What are the dates for this trip? I assume it's a romantic getaway, so you're thinking of rose petals on the bed, maybe moonlit dinners on the beach?"

"Yes, and yes." He nods, and another burst of glitter falls from his hair. "Departure date is this Saturday. I want this to be a honeymoon to remember."

My eyes dart to his left hand, but his ring finger is bare.

Did he get married last night? Is his wife somewhere in the office missing half of her clothes?

I glance over my shoulder at the darkened corridor and closed office doors.

"I know better than to fall asleep in my office chair." He stretches his arms over his head. "My back is fucked."

"You owe a hundred to the fund," I mumble.

"I owe a hell of a lot more than a hundred." He huffs out a chuckle. "You heard me fighting with that glitter cannon, didn't you? I must have let a few choice words escape when it fell on the floor."

I pinch the bridge of my nose. There are enough clues to piece together the mystery of what Keats did last night and this morning, but I don't want to put in the effort.

Maybe this is why Jamie came to work late some days.

Glancing up, I force a smile. "I'll get to work. I'll put together a few options for your honeymoon so you can choose one. Oh, and congratulations to you and your wife."

He laughs, tossing his head back. "What the fuck, Maren? You think I got married?"

"Two hundred," I say while my cheeks bloom pink in embarrassment. "You said I should book a luxury honeymoon. You're dressed in a tuxedo. You didn't have pants on when I got here, and you have an empty bottle of champagne and a glitter cannon in your office."

"Woah." He holds up his palm, and I get a glimpse of something written in black ink.

I tilt my head to read it, but he drops his hand to his side. "I officiated a wedding at midnight. I came back here with the happy couple to notarize their wedding certificate. The groom was carrying a magnum of champagne. He spilled half the fucking bottle on my pants, so I took them off the second the newlyweds left."

I nod, not wanting to say anything to interrupt his train of thought.

He stares at me for a second before he sighs. "I used to keep an extra pair of pants in the cabinet behind my desk. I was looking for those when I found the glitter cannon. It was supposed to be a gift for Stevie's birthday, but my brother told me no way. Anyways, I must have worn the spare pair of pants home one day and forgot to bring them back."

I don't have words, so I keep listening.

He exhales sharply. "I accidentally knocked the cannon out of the cabinet when I was searching for the pants and glitter went everywhere. I kicked it and whatever was left inside of it shot me in the face."

As if on cue, another sprinkle of glitter rains from his hair onto his nose and cheeks.

"I need to get someone in here to clean up that fucking mess." He motions toward the door of his office. "I know, three hundred. I owe three hundred goddamn dollars. Four now."

I bite back a laugh. "So, you're not married?"

His eyes widen. "Heck, no."

Something inside of me relaxes. "How often do you officiate weddings?"

Scrubbing a hand over the back of his neck, he shrugs. "Whenever I need to. The couple I married last night was eager to make it happen before their twins arrive."

"Twins?" I swallow hard. "That's a lot."

"They'll handle it." He half-laughs. "We've been friends since high school. They work at his family's diner on the Lower East Side. I stop in there whenever I'm craving a plate of fries and a greasy cheeseburger."

He swats his hand against his hair to knock more glitter loose. "They've never charged me for a meal, so when Brandi and Chuck said they were planning on heading to City Hall to tie the knot next week, I told them I'd do it whenever they wanted."

"They wanted it immediately?" I smile.

"The sooner the better, they said." He brushes his fingertips over the lapel of his jacket, chasing away some glitter. "They already had their marriage license, so we decided to do it after the diner closed. I went home and threw on my tux. I picked up some flowers on my way back, and sealed the deal at the stroke of midnight."

# CHAPTER TWELVE

*MAREN*

TO THINK I was in bed by ten last night and at that time, Keats was still hours away from officiating a last-minute wedding at a diner. My boss doesn't live a boring life.

"I'm going to run home to shower and change before I get down to business." Keats tosses me a grin. "I'll drop this tux off at the dry cleaners on my way back. I need it next week."

There's a question begging to be asked, but I'm sure in time I'll find out if he's marrying another couple next week or if the need for his tux is because of something else.

"I'll arrange to have your office cleaned," I offer because it's my job and because I haven't forgotten that he's paying me a ridiculous amount of money to be his assistant.

"I think we need to call in some big guns to take care of the glitter cannon clusterfuck in my office. The vacuum cleaner that the building's cleaning crew has is too lightweight for this job."

"You owe another hundred," I shoot back. "I know

someone who will have all of that cleaned up by noon. I'll arrange for it to happen."

"I trust you, so give them a call and get them here as soon as possible."

I slide open my bottom drawer to reach for my phone. "I'll take care of it now."

"I'm going home." He starts back toward his office. "I need to find my shoes."

My gaze wanders to his ass again as he walks away.

Suddenly, he looks back to catch me watching him. "Jamie wouldn't have stepped up to the plate to help me out the way you are, Maren."

All I'm doing is arranging for the cleaning crew who took care of my dad's offices to come down here to de-glitter this place.

"It's my job," I sound back.

"You're doing a he…heck of a good job so far."

I take pride in that even though it's only my second day, and every task I've been assigned so far has been easy.

I watch as he slides his feet into his black wingtip shoes. As he stalks back toward me, his gaze falls to his hand. "What the…?"

His voice trails as he glances at whatever is written on his palm in black ink.

"Is there a problem?" I probe because I want to know what the secret message is.

He turns his hand to face me. I silently read the ten digits of what I assume is a phone number.

"A woman at the club asked for Pace's autograph on her…well, she wanted him to sign her," he stumbles his way through that while circling a finger in front of his chest. "She yanked a marker out of her purse, and then Pace handed it to her friend when he was finished with it."

I nod, realizing what he's about to say.

"The friend grabbed my hand and scribbled something down." Shaking his head, he scrubs at the numbers with his finger. "She told me to use it. I didn't realize until I went to wash my hands that it was her number, and the ink is fucking permanent."

I suck in a breath. "You swore."

"I swore off calling random women who write their phone numbers on my body."

"What?" I ask before I realize the question has left my lips.

"You don't want to know." He chuckles. "I'll get this off at home. Rubbing alcohol will erase it in a flash."

My mouth continues spitting out things I shouldn't say to my boss. "You should save the number to your phone before you do that."

He crosses his arms over his chest. "Why? I have no intention of using the number."

I tilt my chin up. "You don't."

He takes in the green dress I'm wearing before his gaze settles on my face. "No. I don't."

Since I'm the one who led us into awkward territory, I guide us out. "I'll call the cleaners."

His eyes lock on mine. "I appreciate you helping me with this."

I nod. "If there's anything else I can do for you today, please let me know."

"Have dinner with me."

I open my mouth to refuse, but I don't get a word in.

"I set up a meeting with Fletcher Newman tonight," he goes on. "He's a potential new client. I want you to be there."

*It's a work dinner.*

Regardless of what I feel, I can't refuse to show up. "Let me know when and where, and I'll be there."

"I'll text you the details as soon as I'm cleaned up." He motions toward the elevator. "I'm going to get the heck out of here before anyone else shows up."

I glance at the watch on my wrist. He needs to hurry. My colleagues will be arriving at any minute.

"I'll be back in a couple of hours," he calls over his shoulder as he sprints to the elevator. "If anyone needs me, tell them to sit tight. And if Pace calls, hang up on him."

I let out a laugh. "I'll talk to him."

After jabbing a finger into the elevator call button, he turns to face me. "He's bad news. You're too good for him, Maren."

Before I can ask what he means by that, the elevator doors slide open, and Everett appears.

"Is that glitter on your face, boss?" he asks with amusement in his tone.

Keats moves around him to board the elevator just as Everett steps off. "What do you think?"

With that, the doors slide shut, and Everett turns to face me. "Do I want to know what the hell that's about? Or do I file it under Keats being Keats?"

I laugh. "Is Keats covered in glitter a regular thing?"

"That part is new." He laughs. "So is that extra bounce in his step. You must have something to do with that, Maren."

Office gossip is the last thing I need, so I shut it down with a shake of my head. "I'm only here to clean up the messes."

Everett looks past me to the glitter-covered floor of Keats's office. "Good luck with that."

# CHAPTER THIRTEEN

*KEATS*

WHAT'S that bullshit about the best-laid plans?

I had my day planned out to the last second, but that was blown to hell when Berk called as I stepped out of the shower. He asked if I could watch Stevie because she had a mild fever when she woke up, and he didn't want to send her to school. The regular sitter had an appointment booked. I'm next on the list, so I lucked out.

Instead of spending my day chasing after new clients, I played video games with my niece while she teased me about the glitter she saw in my ear. I cooked a frozen pizza I found in Berk's freezer for lunch, and I sneezed my way through Sully taking a nap in my lap before I piggybacked Stevie to my townhouse for the afternoon.

Berk would have taken the day off to be with his daughter, but he had a meeting with Nicholas Wolf and his agent. The novelist is looking for a new publishing house to work with, and

Berk made the shortlist. I'm proud to say that my friendship with Nicholas's brother, Liam, played a part in that. Signing Nicholas would take Berk's business to the next level. I want that for him.

I told my brother to make sure he got his ass home before six because I have plans at seven. Once he assured me he'd be home at least two hours before that, I sent Maren a text telling her she had the day off.

I told her to meet me at Nova at quarter to seven.

Securing a table at one of the most popular restaurants in Manhattan at such short notice is easy when you're friends with the owner. Tyler Monroe launched Nova a few years ago, and it's found its niche in the crowded culinary market of New York City.

It never hurts to have connections in the hospitality industry when you make a living wining and dining elite athletes.

"I wish someone would convince my dad to get me a phone." Stevie tosses me some serious side-eye from where she's curled up in a chair next to the fireplace.

She made a mad dash for the library as soon as she kicked off her sneakers after we bolted inside.

In addition to this library and the massive living room with attached dining room, this townhouse has a chef's kitchen, three bedrooms, two bathrooms, and a self-contained one bedroom unit on the upper floor.

I purchased it when Layna was first diagnosed because I thought my brother and his family could live on the lower two floors while I took up residence on the top floor. I wanted them close.

It never dawned on me that Berk would use the money he inherited from our grandfather to buy a townhouse a few blocks away. Layna had a dream to decorate her own home, so Berk made it happen. He moved his family out of the cramped two-bedroom apartment they were renting.

They made memories in the five-bedroom home that Berk and Stevie live in now.

Living on the Upper West Side in a house that's way too fucking big for me was never on my life's plan list, but I like it here.

Stevie drops her gaze to the Hemingway book in her hands. I stocked up on short stories about zombies and curious kid detectives, but Stevie always goes for the classics when she visits me.

I have no idea if she's reading the book or admiring the dust jacket.

"Your dad said no to a phone because he thinks you're too young," I remind her. "Give it a few months and then ask him again."

She turns to face me. "If you asked him for me, he might say yes."

"In what universe would Berk say yes to me and not you?" I lean back into the soft leather of the couch I'm sitting on.

"He said yes when you wanted to buy me a piano."

This kid has an answer to everything, and in this instance, she's right.

"I wanted to teach you how to play," I point out. "Your dad was pissed that you snuck out and came here to practice, so I had to buy you a piano, Stevie."

"You swore." A smile brightens her face. "You owe a hundred to our charity."

*Our charity.*

There isn't an eight-year-old kid on this earth who should be as invested in raising money for an organization as Stevie is. The Layna Morgan Foundation is co-run by Layna's parents and my brother. It offers financial help to women battling cancer.

I have no doubt that Stevie will be at the helm as soon as she's legally old enough.

"I'm good for it." I smile.

She bounces her foot in the air. "Do you think I'll always remember her?"

My gaze wanders to a framed picture of Berk, Layna, and Stevie on the mantle. It was taken a year before Layna died. "You'll always remember her."

"Do you think daddy will fall in love again one day?"

The word *no* almost leaves my mouth, but miracles happen, so I shrug. "You never know."

Berk refuses to talk about dating, so I stopped bringing it up. Stevie asked once, and her dad avoided the question. She took the hint that it was a topic he won't discuss. I'm the one she looks to for answers about her dad's future.

"I'm getting married when I'm thirty, so I can't live with him forever. I don't want him to be lonely when I move out."

"Who the heck are you marrying?" I question with a perk of both brows.

She tugs on one of the sleeves of the pink sweatshirt she's wearing. "A doctor. I haven't met him yet, but I will. We'll work together. I'll take care of the pet patients, and he'll take care of the people patients."

This kid's life plan is next level.

"Your dad will get you a phone by then so you can check in on him." I grin. "There's hope on the horizon, Stevie. You'll get that phone eventually."

She rolls her big blue eyes. "I can't wait that long."

My gaze drops to my phone when it buzzes. I read a quick text from my brother asking how Stevie is. I punch out a reply telling him that her fever is gone.

"Will you ever get married?"

I drop the phone on my lap. "Me?"

"You're the only one here." Stevie tucks a lock of her brown hair behind her ear. "Why don't you get married, Keats?"

"Why don't you read that book?" I try to change the subject.

I'm rewarded with another exaggerated eye roll from my niece. "You're going to be thirty soon. Isn't part of your plan to be married by then?"

At one point in the not-too-distant past, I thought it was part of my plan, but life has a way of knocking you off course. In my case, reality slapped me across the face and kicked my ass at the same time.

"I only plan short-term, and right now, I'm planning on a piano lesson before your dad comes home from work."

Stevie bounces to her feet. "I'll race you to the piano."

Before I'm standing, she's on her way down the hallway, headed toward the corner of the living room where the piano awaits.

"The loser is the winner," I call out.

That spins her around to face me. She leans her back against the wall. "After you, Keats. My dad says I need to respect older people, so you should lead the way."

"Funny," I set off at a sprint past her. "Rule change. The winner is the winner."

She falls in step next to me, gives me an elbow shove, and takes off down the hallway, laughing as she runs.

## CHAPTER FOURTEEN

*MAREN*

"HOW WAS your second day at your new job?" Arietta asks innocently as she pats Dudley's head. "I didn't think you'd beat me home today."

I shift my gaze back to the screen of my laptop. "I've been home for hours."

I hear the shuffle of Arietta's sensible shoes against the floor as she approaches me. "Did something happen? Did you get F. I. R. E. D?"

A laugh bubbles out of me. "Why did you spell that?"

She lets out a heavy sigh as she drops her purse on the couch next to me. "I don't know. To soften the blow, maybe?"

"I still have a J. O. B." I smile. "Keats took the day off to take care of his sick niece, so he told me to go home."

"Is she okay?" Concern settles in Arietta's expression.

I've never met anyone as empathetic as her. On the odd day I get a migraine, Arietta has a headache within the hour. She feels other people's pain deeply, maybe too deeply.

"He didn't sound concerned on the call." I glance at the screen of my laptop again. "I'll ask for an update on his niece when I meet him for dinner."

I know better than to toss information like that at Arietta with no other explanation, but I know her reaction will bring a smile to my face.

"Wait? What?" She lets her hair down from the tight bun she wound it into this morning. Her golden locks bounce around her shoulders as she shakes her head back-and-forth. "Are you going on a date with your boss?"

"If you had the chance, you'd go on a date with your boss," I counter.

Ever since I briefly met Dominick Calvetti, I've teased Arietta about him. His face and body should be plastered on a billboard, advertising cologne, or expensive clothing. He's gorgeous.

Arietta always scoffs when I mention his name. I can tell by the grimace on her face that she's about to tell me he's not her type. "You know I don't like him, Maren."

"You love him, "I singsong. "Arietta Calvetti. How perfect does that sound?"

She playfully presses her hands to her stomach. "I think I may vomit."

I snap the cover of my laptop shut. "Aim for the floor."

With a laugh, she drops on the couch next to me. "You didn't answer my question. Are you going on a date with Mr. Morgan?"

I set my laptop on the coffee table. "It's a business dinner. He's meeting a potential new client. It's a baseball player. I was just researching him."

Her gaze volleys between the closed laptop and my face. "What are you going to wear to this business dinner?"

I trail a finger over her shoulder. "I was hoping I could borrow your outfit."

The corners of her lips curl up. "I know you're teasing."

I am. Arietta's ensemble of the day consists of a yellow dress that's at least two sizes too big and a purple cardigan covered in red butterflies.

"You should wear that red lace dress you bought last month." She jumps to her feet. "And your red strappy heels. They make your legs look ten feet long."

"Do I want that?"

"You're a model without a runway, Maren." She darts her hands to her hips. "I'll do your makeup."

That's an offer I won't turn down. Arietta has serious makeup application skills for someone who only wears the bare minimum of mascara and pale pink lipstick.

I move to stand. "You don't think the red dress is too much for a business dinner?"

"It's perfect. It's sophisticated with a hint of sexy." Her hand tugs on a lock of my hair. "There's something about a redhead in a red dress that drives men wild."

Tilting my head, I perk a brow. "I'm not trying to drive any men wild tonight, Arietta."

She laughs. "Do you expect me to believe that, Mrs. Morgan."

"Touché," I say with a muted chuckle. "That will never happen. Keats Morgan is a handful."

Her gaze narrows. "Is that a bad thing?"

"It's very bad." I point toward the hallway. "It's time for me to get ready. Work your magic."

---

I'M EARLY FOR EVERYTHING. I always have been.

When I was in second grade, my dad would walk me to school thirty minutes before class was scheduled to start so I could be first in line once the bell rang, signaling the start of the day.

I don't fear being late, but I believe there's value in always being on time.

People appreciate it when you're punctual, so I made sure I left my apartment with more than enough time to spare. I didn't want to be even a second late to my first business dinner with Keats.

I left Dudley in Arietta's care with a promise that I'd bring her back something decadent for dessert.

In the envelope that contained my contract, there was a business card for a car service. I'm permitted to use them as long as the trip is related to work. I considered calling them tonight, but that seemed like a lot of trouble to get from Tribeca to Greenwich Village.

I hopped on the subway before I walked the last block to Nova.

I skim my hand over the skirt of my red dress as I approach the restaurant's entrance.

This isn't my first time here. My dad decided he wanted to celebrate Father's Day with a meal fit for a king, so I booked a table for three. It was one of the best dinners we've ever had. The food was a close second to the company. I love spending time with my parents. Our relationship has always been close, but there's been a gradual shift as I've grown up.

I wouldn't say we're friends, but I consider them the two most important people in my life, even though they keep asking if I have a boyfriend.

I smile at a man in a black suit greeting people at the door. He grabs the handle and swings it open for me. "Welcome to Nova."

I grin back. "Thank you."

I survey the interior of the restaurant. It's busy. People are seated near the bar, and from my vantage point, it looks as though every table is occupied.

Panic strikes me as I suddenly wonder if I was supposed to book a reservation. I look at the text Keats sent me earlier to double-check that I didn't miss anything.

"Maren Weber? Is that you?"

I wince when I hear the voice behind me. It can't be. There's no way in hell that Christian Knott is here.

Maybe if I ignore him, he'll go away.

"That's her, and she looks incredible."

The second voice has a rasp to it that sends a pulse straight through me. I shouldn't react to it the way I do, but Keats has a voice that can send goose bumps trailing up a woman's arms.

It's happening to me right now.

"I'm Keats Morgan," he says from behind me. "Who are you?"

I turn to face them both because there's no denying that I can hear their conversation.

"I'm the man who may be persuaded to give Maren a second chance." Christian chuckles.

*Jerk.*

Since we're standing in the entrance to a crowded restaurant, I keep that comment to myself. Shaking my head, I clear my throat.

Keats looks at Christian as if he's studying his expensive suit and perfectly styled brown hair. "You're an idiot."

Christian's brow furrows. "Excuse me?"

Keats steps closer to me. I'm hit with the masculine scent of his cologne. Or is that him? Whatever it is, it's intoxicating.

"Did you call me an idiot?" Christian's voice jumps in volume.

"I did." Keats nods his head. "You had a chance with Maren and blew it. That's an idiot move."

I realize what's happening immediately. Keats thinks I was involved with Christian. *Ew. Just ew.*

"We never." I reach for Keats's forearm. "Christian wasn't my boyfriend. I don't have a boyfriend. He fired me."

Keats's gaze scans my face. "He fired you?"

I nod. "Last week. It was the day I found Dudley."

The corners of Keats's mouth curl up in a sexy smile. He turns his attention back to Christian. "My mistake."

"Are you sorry you called me an idiot?" Christian smirks.

Keats lets out a laugh. "I had it wrong. You're more of an asshole than an idiot. If you'll excuse us, we have a reservation."

Christian's hand lands on Keats's shoulder. "You think I'm an asshole?"

Keats swats Christian's hand away with his own. "I know you are. I doubt like hell there was anything Maren did to warrant termination."

Christian takes a step back. Unease settles over his expression. I know that look. Keats hit a nerve. "That's between Maren and me."

Keats crosses his arms. "Fair enough. Your loss is my gain."

"She works for you now?"

"She does," Keats answers curtly.

Christian huffs out a laugh. "Good luck with that, man. You're going to need it."

## CHAPTER FIFTEEN

*Keats*

IF I WERE A TWELVE-YEAR-OLD, I would have decked Christian Knott with a swift punch to the nose. Berk taught me how to defend myself when a kid who was four inches taller and twenty pounds heavier than me decided I'd be his unwilling victim.

He was a bully. I was scared shitless of him until Berk showed me how to land a punch designed to break noses. I didn't accomplish that when my fist hit the center of the bully's face, but I did manage to knock him sideways.

That was my one and only attempt to defend myself physically. Since then, I've learned that assholes hate being called out for who they are. That's especially true if a beautiful woman is within earshot.

I know all about Christian Knott. Everett handed me a copy of the job application Maren filled out the day I hired her. I wanted to be sure that she did, in fact, have the qualifications for the job.

She's overqualified, but the point is that the Knott brothers lost a valued employee.

I don't know the specifics of what happened. I do know that she works for me now. I intend to keep it that way.

"I'm sorry about that," she says from her seat next to me.

We were directed to the bar to wait for our table after Christian took off. I have an eye trained on the door, so I can spot Fletcher when he arrives and Christian if he shows his face in here again.

I didn't expect to run into anyone Maren knows tonight. I wanted a drink before dinner, so I arrived at Nova early. To my surprise, my new assistant was already here. I saw her through the window before I noticed creepy Christian sneaking up behind her.

That's when I made my way inside.

I pegged Christian as an ex-boyfriend at first, because he couldn't take his eyes off of her ass. Then Maren mentioned his name. If I had cared more, I might have looked him up online days ago, but stalking my employees' former bosses isn't something I do.

The past is the past, whether it's jobs or lovers.

"For what?" I laugh. "You're not responsible for that asshole."

Her eyes brighten. "You swore."

I drag my tongue over my bottom lip. "I did. You're right."

Her gaze stays trained on my mouth before it travels slowly to my eyes. "He made it sound as though I'm a difficult employee."

"What he says is irrelevant." I reach for the glass of scotch in front of me. "You're proving to be a valuable addition to our team."

The words don't convey the message. I like working with

CATCH 71

this woman. I love sitting here while she sips on a glass of red wine, and I stare at her beautiful face.

"He fired me because I pushed back on a decision he made." She sighs. "He passed me over for a promotion. He gave the position to someone close to him."

"Fucking asshole." I smile. "It was worth the money to say it."

That lures a laugh from her.

I watch as she giggles her way through a hiccup.

"I sometimes hiccup when I laugh," she explains before her body jerks with another hiccup. "I hope it passes before Fletcher gets here."

I hope to hell it doesn't. It's fucking adorable. With each hiccup, her hair bounces, and her eyes widen.

"Maybe if I drink this, it will help." The words pour out of her quickly before she downs half the glass of wine.

As soon as she sets it back on the bar, a hiccup escapes her.

"Dammit." Her eyes search my face. "I know this meeting is important. I can't have the hiccups right now."

I'd tell her it doesn't matter, but I can sense that it matters a hell of a lot to her, so I offer my advice, even though she never asked. "Press the thumb of your right hand into the middle of your left palm."

"What?" Her hands fall open on her lap.

My gaze drifts from them down to her legs. *Jesus, those legs.* They could make a man forget his name.

"Keats," she offers me a reminder she didn't know I needed. "Where on my palm do I press?"

Her left hand reaches out to me, and damn if I'm going to pass over the opportunity to touch her.

When the pad of my thumb touches the middle of her palm, I almost moan. What the hell is wrong with me? I suck in a deep breath. I need to calm down. For fuck's sake, I need to calm down.

A hiccup jolts her. "Please press it for me."

I lock eyes with her as I cup her hand between mine. I gently press into the middle of her left palm as I stare at her. "It's the best way I know to chase hiccups away."

Uncertainty swims in her expression, but she doesn't move as she hiccups again.

"I learned how to do this when I was a kid," I explain. "Whenever I had a soda, I'd get the hiccups."

The corners of her lips quirk up toward a grin. "You did?"

I don't take my eyes off of her. "I couldn't drink a soda at a birthday party because I'd have to hiccup my way through the birthday song."

Her right hand jumps to her mouth as she stifles a laugh followed by a hiccup. "I bet the birthday boy or girl loved that."

I chuckle. "The first time it happened, every kid there joined in and fake hiccupped along with me."

She lowers her hand to her chin. "So, someone taught you how to get rid of hiccups because of that?"

I apply more pressure to her palm. "My grandfather did. The man had a pocketful of tricks just like this one."

Her gaze drops to our hands before it levels back on my face. "What else did he teach you?"

I lean closer to her because the volume in this place just went up a notch. "He was the king of life hacks before they were a thing."

She leans in too. "Tell me one. I want to learn something new."

*I like you. I really fucking like you.*

The thought stays inside of me because that's not a life hack. It's a fact of life.

"Wear a hoodie backward when you're watching a movie. You have a built-in container for popcorn."

She narrows her eyes. "You use the hood to hold the popcorn? Have you done that?"

"More than once, " I admit. "I taught Stevie to do it too. It's a family tradition."

Leaning closer, she laughs. "Why do I get the impression that you're a bad influence on her?"

I don't take that as anything but a compliment. The smile on Maren's face tells me she meant it in jest. "You can ask her if I am when you meet her."

"I'll meet her?" she questions.

"I'd like you to," I lower my voice. "And my brother too."

She doesn't say a word, so I keep talking. "Jamie used to drop by my townhouse for dinner sometimes. Everett and his wife do too. Everyone who has worked for me has been to my home."

Whatever reservation may have been holding back her response is gone. With a soft smile, she looks into my eyes. "I'd love to meet your family, Keats."

"I told you Mr. Morgan was a decent guy, Dad."

Maren and I both turn at the sound of my name.

*Goddammit.* I took my eyes off the restaurant's entrance and missed my chance to greet a potential client who could change my life.

"You called him a party boy." Fletcher Newman lets out a gruff laugh as he elbows his father. "Mr. Morgan is going to introduce his girlfriend to his family. It looks like you had him all wrong."

# CHAPTER SIXTEEN

*MAREN*

I YANK my hand free of Keats's grip. I look to him to correct Fletcher's assumption, but that doesn't happen. Instead, Keats jumps to his feet and offers his hand to Fletcher's father.

"Mr. Newman, I'm glad you decided to join us."

Mr. Newman takes Keats's hand for an abrupt shake. "When Fletcher mentioned that he was having dinner with you, I wasn't about to let him come alone. There is a reason we haven't returned your calls, Mr. Morgan."

*Ouch. Talk about not-so-subtle shade.*

Keats doesn't flinch. Instead, he addresses the comment head-on. "I assume you're talking about my reputation."

The farthest I dove into Keats's reputation was reading the responses to my post about Dudley.

When I did an online search for Keats that night, I honed in on his business website. I bypassed the image gallery that popped up and all the gossip sites.

"It's not squeaky clean." Mr. Newman sighs. "There are

pictures and stories online. Word gets around between players."

Keats rubs his chin. "I can't say I've been an angel in the past, sir."

"What are you now?" Mr. Newman shifts his attention to me. "Has he changed?"

Since I've known him for less than a week, I don't feel qualified to pass judgment. I do feel I should say something about who I am to Keats.

"Of course, he's changed." Fletcher laughs. He pushes his blond hair back from his forehead. "He just asked his girlfriend to meet his family. Didn't you do that with mom right before you proposed?"

My body tenses. How did we go from the Newmans assuming I'm Keats's girlfriend to talking about marriage?

I finish the last of the wine in my glass.

"If he's settling down, I might be inclined to stay for dinner," Mr. Newman says to Fletcher before he looks at Keats. "I don't want my son represented by someone who is going to drag him to parties every night. His agent has to lead by example."

I'm tempted to interrupt to tell my boss to cut his losses now.

"No party dragging will be happening tonight," Keats jokes.

Mr. Newman doesn't crack a smile. "Give me a reason to stay and hear you out, Mr. Morgan. We're both aware of how promising my son's future is."

I lock eyes with Fletcher for the briefest of moments. I read his bio. He just turned twenty-one two months ago. When I was that age, my parents tried to steer me in the right direction, but they let me hold the wheel. Alone.

I realize that Fletcher's future is at stake. Choosing the right agent can make or break his career.

"He represents Pace. Isn't that enough?" Fletcher asks, looking at his dad.

Mr. Newman shakes his head. "Pace Callahan's ringing endorsement isn't enough for me."

I watch Keats suck in a deep breath. I may not know a lot about his business, but I do know that he wants to represent Fletcher. If he weren't good at his job, he wouldn't have so many top athletes as clients.

"Is my ringing endorsement enough?" I ask quietly.

Mr. Newman turns to face me head-on. "I'm sure you're a lovely young woman, but this is between us men."

That snaps Keats's gaze in my direction. Before I have a chance to open my mouth, Keats opens his. "Excuse me? What did you say to her?"

I rest a hand on Keats's forearm because I can fight my own battles. I win most.

"We're going to talk business." Mr. Fletcher tosses me a look. "Your date doesn't need to be present for that."

"Maren is a lot more than a date." Keats buttons his jacket. "She's an educated, intelligent, compassionate woman who deserves respect. If you view her as anything less than that, we need to end this conversation now."

Stunned, I glance at Keats to catch him looking at me. He offers me a smile, so I return one.

*Did he just throw his chance to represent Fletcher under the bus to defend my honor?*

"Dad," Fletcher snaps. "Don't do this."

Mr. Newman steals a glance at his son before he pats Keats on the shoulder. "Any man who steps up to the plate like that for the woman he loves is a man I want in my son's corner."

Keats looks as stunned as I feel. He shakes his head. "What?"

Mr. Newman turns to me. "Please forgive me for that, Maren. You can tell a lot about a man's character by how he responds in certain situations. I wanted to see what your man was made of."

*Keats is not my man.*

Those words sit on the tip of my tongue because I'm still in shock over the fact that Mr. Newman thinks my boss is in love with me.

I'm here for business. Someone needs to say it. I look at Keats, but his gaze is volleying between Fletcher and his dad.

"He was willing to walk away for you." Mr. Newman grins. "He's not the man I thought he was. I was under the impression that Keats Morgan was a self-absorbed, irresponsible, cocky bastard. I'm glad I was wrong."

Keats must take that as a twisted compliment because he only nods in response.

I feel as though we've fallen into a hole that is so deep we can't crawl out.

Fletcher confirms that when he slaps Keats on the back. "It looks like we're staying for dinner. You should tell my dad all about how you and Maren met. He's a big softie when it comes to love stories."

# CHAPTER SEVENTEEN

***Keats***

I'VE JUMPED onto a runaway train, and I'm holding on by my fingertips for my fucking life. I should grab the brake and drag this screaming hot mess of a misunderstanding to a screeching stop, but I don't.

Maren has to think I'm a no-good, deceitful asshole by now.

I can't tell what's going on in her head because she's been engrossed in a conversation with Earl Newman for the past fifteen minutes. He asked how we met and she skillfully shifted the topic to France without answering his question. Fletcher's dad loosened up as soon as he took his first sip of the imported French beer he ordered on Maren's recommendation.

I opted for sparkling water because if my reputation is in question, I'm playing it safe.

Fletcher followed my lead. Maren chose another glass of red wine to complement the steak she ordered.

"There is a reason that people say you should visit Paris in the spring," Maren says, and Earl eats it up like a kid with an ice cream cone.

The gray-haired accountant has a mad crush on my assistant. I don't know whether to be grateful for that or jealous of it.

Clearing my throat, I glance in the direction of the kitchen. I have at least a few minutes before our meals arrive. "Tell me how you envision your future, Fletcher."

Earl tosses me a look that could melt the sun. Dammit. Is he pissed that I interrupted his gabfest with Maren? I hope to hell this doesn't result in a penalty. I want to represent Fletcher, and the route to that goal is through his father.

"The majors, I guess." He shrugs.

I wouldn't be here otherwise. This kid has more potential than Pace did when I met him. Fletcher is going to be on the roster of a major league team within the next six months. It's a miracle he hasn't signed with another agent yet.

"You're not the only guy in town who can make that happen." Earl loosens the blue tie around his neck.

The Newmans arrived in matching outfits. Dark blue pants, white button-down shirts, and light blue ties.

"True, but you're not looking for just any guy. You're searching for the best guy." I sit back in my chair.

Maren turns to me with raised brows. She might think it's all talk, but I believe every fucking word of it.

"We want someone who envisions the big picture to represent Fletcher." Earl takes a sip of beer. "Look what happened to Pace Callahan. His career is over just like that."

To accentuate the point, Earl snaps his fingers.

"His career isn't over," Maren pipes up. "Keats negotiated a lucrative deal that will jumpstart a new venture for Pace. You'll be hearing an announcement very soon."

She tosses me a glance, and I nod. I like that she stepped in and that she was vague with details. I'm surprised Pace hasn't rented a billboard in Times Square to announce his new assignment. That might be worth looking into. Anything I can do to up his exposure will equal more money in the coffers when I revisit that deal two years from now.

"You know Pace?" Fletcher leans both elbows on the table. "I talked to him on the phone for ten minutes. Have you met him in person?"

Maren nods. "We had coffee together yesterday."

"No shit?" Fletcher laughs.

"No shit," I repeat with a grin.

Maren's gaze swings toward me. "That's a hundred to the fund."

Before I can comment, she grimaces and mouths the words, "*I'm sorry.*"

Earl laughs. "Did you just take him to task for cursing? He needs to hand over a hundred dollars to a swear jar?"

"Keats is determined not to swear around his niece, so every time he curses, he's penalized a hundred dollars. The money is donated to charity once a month," Maren explains without looking at me.

"Really?" Earl's eyes narrow. "I admit I had you wrong, Keats. I'm proof that the love of a good woman can change a man for the better. It looks like you are proof of that too."

This is another chance for me to stop this shitshow in its path, but I don't. I watch Maren's shoulders as they tense.

"Why don't we stop by your office tomorrow and meet your team?" Earl loosens his tie again. "I can make time later in the day. Are you free at around four?"

"I'm free." I nod.

Earl's gaze wanders to the left. "It looks like dinner is about to be served. I'm glad we had this opportunity to talk,

Maren. Is there any chance you'll be visiting Keats at his office tomorrow? I'd love for my wife to meet you."

With a fleeting glance over her shoulder, Maren sends me a silent message with a perk of her brow. She's asking what the hell should she say.

I step in to handle it, even though I have no fucking clue how this got out of control so fast. "Maren and I work together."

Earl leans back as the server places a plate filled with seafood in front of him. "I had no idea."

Fletcher whistles at the steak and vegetables he ordered. "Look at this feast. We should have dinner again tomorrow after we come to the office."

"We can't," Earl says to his son as he pushes a shrimp around on his plate. "We're meeting up with Buck Remsen and his son for dinner after we stop by Keats's office."

*For fuck's sake.*

There's no way in hell I'm letting Finn Remsen and his old man steal Fletcher away from me.

I'm on good terms with most of my competition, but the Remsens and I have a complicated relationship. Finn and I went to high school together. We were close until we decided to pursue the same career path. Since then, we've been toe-to-toe battling it out for the same clients.

His dad, Buck, represents some of the biggest names in sports. Finn jumped on board after college to help his dad out.

"It's time to eat." Earl taps the handle of his fork against the table. "Here's to a satisfying meal. This may not be Paris, but the food looks just as good."

*Dude. You're married. Stop with the flirting.*

I take a bite of bread to swallow those words with. I need to keep it together. I didn't come this far not to sign Fletcher Newman.

Maren leans closer to me as Earl comments to his son about the food. "What just happened?"

Tilting my head so my lips almost touch her ear, I whisper. "I messed up. I'm sorry you were dragged into this."

She turns toward me. Her eyes lock on mine. "I could have said something."

"This isn't on you, Maren."

"He's important to you, isn't he?" She dips her chin. "Fletcher is."

I nod.

She glances at Earl. "We'll make it happen. You're going to be Fletcher's agent and I'm going to do whatever I can to make that happen."

## CHAPTER EIGHTEEN

*MAREN*

I DON'T KNOW if it was the two glasses of wine, or the fact that I could feel Keats's breath skirting over my cheek, but I fell under a spell last night. That's the only explanation I can think of for why I told my boss that I'd do anything to help him sign Fletcher.

After Keats paid the check and we said our goodbyes to the Newmans, I hurried out of Nova.

I needed air.

I walked into the restaurant expecting a buttoned-up business dinner. I walked out as Keats Morgan's girlfriend. At least, that's who I am to Fletcher Newman and his father.

There's no way that this can end well.

Morning light brought a mild hangover along with a dash of reality. We can't continue this ruse. If Keats signs a contract with Fletcher, it won't take long before the Newmans realize that my relationship with Keats is business only.

"That's the third outfit you've tried on," Arietta says from the doorway of my bedroom. She's still dressed in gray sweatpants and a white T-shirt. I'm not surprised since it's not even seven a.m. yet.

Dudley is in her arms, wrapped in a pink blanket that was in the box with his things. It's not that cold out. The puppy doesn't need to be swaddled.

"Is he all right?" I point toward Dudley.

"He likes to snuggle in the morning." Arietta plants a kiss next to his ear. "He crawls into bed with me before the break of dawn."

That's suspicious since I put him in his kennel each night and close the door.

"Don't fall in love with him, Arietta," I warn.

"I told you I don't like my boss." She rolls her eyes. "I admit he's attractive, but when he opens his mouth, it's all ugly from there. He's bossy, which makes sense given he's my boss, but it wouldn't kill him to say something nice to me occasionally."

Adjusting the front of the white blouse I'm wearing, I laugh. "I was talking about Dudley, but it's good to know you think Dominick is hot."

Her eyes widen behind her glasses. "I didn't say that."

"You did." I wink. "I won't tell him."

Shaking her head, she half-laughs. "Promise?"

"If you help me with my makeup, I promise never to tell Mr. Calvetti that you have a crush on him."

"I don't," she states with a grin. "And I will help with your makeup, but I'm curious about something."

I save her the trouble of asking by explaining why I'm putting so much effort into getting ready for work today. "That baseball player I told you about last night is coming by the office today with his dad."

Arietta gently places Dudley in the center of my bed,

tucking the pink blanket under his chin to make a small pillow. He lowers his head down as he watches her cross the room toward me.

"So do you like the ballplayer or his dad?" she questions as she nears me.

"Neither."

Her eyes narrow. "Is it Mr. Morgan? Do you want to look extra nice for him?"

I stare at her reflection in the mirror we're facing. "You've always told me that getting involved with your boss is a bad idea, Arietta."

I haven't told her that I know from personal experience, that it's a fucking terrible idea.

She rests a hand on my forearm. "That's because my boss is a tyrant. I sense that Keats isn't like that."

I hold back a smile. "I wouldn't call him a tyrant."

Arietta takes a half-step to the left so she's standing side-by-side with me. She tugs on the bottom of her sweatshirt. "Would you call him handsome?"

"He's average."

Her face lights up with a megawatt smile. "Average? I saw a few pictures of him online, Maren. He's not average."

I turn to face her. "You think he's handsome?"

She reaches to straighten the waistband of the red pencil skirt I'm wearing. "So do you. Admit it."

I can't deny it so I nod. "He's good-looking."

"You're blushing." She circles a finger in front of my face. "You like him, don't you?"

I ignore that and drop my hands to my hips. "If I wear my red heels, is this the winner?"

She rakes me from head-to-toe. "It's the winner and if Keats Morgan is the man for you, this outfit is going to knock his pants off."

"Socks off," I correct her.

"No." Shaking her head, she pushes her glasses up the bridge of her nose. "The other two outfits you tried on would have knocked his socks off. This will knock his pants off."

I tilt my head as I stare at my reflection. "I'll go with this."

"Take a seat on the chair, and I'll work my makeup magic." Arietta gestures to a gray armchair in the corner of my bedroom. "Mr. Morgan is about to be wowed by his assistant."

## CHAPTER NINETEEN

***KEATS***

"YOU ONLY COME HERE for breakfast for two reasons." My brother eyes me over the mug of coffee perched close to his mouth.

"The first is that I love you," I say with a straight face. "The second is that I love your daughter more."

Berk huffs out a laugh. "Try food or women."

"I've tried both," I quip. "If I had to choose, it would be food. Your pancakes, to be exact."

My brother jerks a thumb toward the pantry in his kitchen. "Help yourself. I ate a bowl of cereal an hour ago. Stevie's breakfast choice as of late is overnight oats and smoothies. If you want pancakes, you're on your own."

I drop onto one of the stools next to the massive granite topped island. "There was a time when you used to cook for me. You didn't want to see me go hungry."

Berk crosses the kitchen to pour a mug of coffee. On this way back toward me, he scoops an apple into his hand from a wicker basket. Both are placed in front of me. "Here's your breakfast. Stop fucking whining."

I bite into the apple. "You owe a hundred to the fund."

With his mug back in his hand, he takes a sip of coffee. "Why the hell are you here at this hour?"

"You're up to two hundred now," I point out. "It's after seven. Aren't you the guy who always brags that he's up by six a.m.?"

"That wasn't an invitation for you to show up here." He shoves his hand in my direction. "Give me back the keys, Keats. If you're going to barge in here whenever you damn well feel like it, I'm going to decide whether I let you in."

I pick up the keys and dangle them in the air. "You can't take them back. Besides, I didn't want to ring the bell. It would have woken Stevie up."

Berk nods. "You can keep the keys, but only because I saw you creeping outside the house on the doorbell cam, so I knew you were on your way in."

I shove the keys into the back pocket of my jeans. "Aren't you glad I had that security system installed for you?"

When I had one installed in my townhouse, I decided Berk and Layna needed the same system. He scoffed at the idea at first, telling me that the Upper West Side is safe.

It is, but having the ability to open an app on your phone and talk to whoever the hell is ringing your doorbell is priceless. I had a ten minute conversation with a pizza delivery driver last year as he stood in the pouring rain on my stoop. I told him I didn't order the five large pies in his hands. He insisted that I did.

I was right since I was lazing on a beach in the Caribbean at the time.

I felt sorry for the guy, so I paid electronically for the

food and a tip. I sent him here to deliver dinner to my brother and his daughter.

Whoever the hell ordered that food missed out. Berk said it was some of the best pizza he's ever had.

"I appreciate that," Berk concedes. "I still want to know why you're here."

"Maren," I say her name to him for the first time.

He tugs on the bottom of his blue T-shirt. I suspect I interrupted him mid-workout judging by the shorts he's wearing and the fact that sweat was dripping from his forehead when he confronted me in the hallway.

Berk converted one of the bedrooms into a mini home gym so he can spend more time with Stevie. He cherishes every second he has with that kid. I do too.

"Maren," he repeats her name. "That's pretty."

"She's pretty." The words fly out before I can stop and think.

My brother's curiosity is piqued. I see it in the way the corners of his lips curve up and the tilt of his chin. "Tell me about Maren."

"Who?" Stevie rounds the corner dressed in dark jeans and a colorful sweater emblazoned with a unicorn picture. On her feet are the sneakers I bought her last month. They're white with pink polka dots.

"My assistant." I look to my brother for his reaction.

Both of his brows arch. "Maren is your assistant."

"Wow." Stevie starts toward the fridge. "I like her name. What is she like?"

*Home.*

I chase that away because where the fuck did that come from?

"She's smart," I answer honestly.

Stevie glances over her shoulder at me. "Smart is good. What else?"

"Maren is kind," I offer. "She's taking care of Dudley."

"I need to meet her." Stevie places a small mason jar filled with something that looks slimy on the counter. "I want to see Duds."

I watch as my niece unscrews the lid of the jar before she plops a spoon into the mess inside.

"Are you going to eat that?" I lean back on my stool.

With a nod, she shoves a spoonful into her mouth. "Daddy makes the best overnight oats ever."

Berk tosses me a look. "You should try them sometime, Keats."

I push back to stand. "Hard pass."

"Are you going to work dressed like that?" Stevie takes in my jeans and hooded sweatshirt.

I lift my chin. "What's wrong with what I'm wearing?"

"If you were in my class, I'd say nothing, but you're an adult."

I spin in a circle. "I'm the boss. I can wear what I want."

That earns me an eye roll. "Wear your dark blue suit with the pink silk tie. And those brown shoes that are on the second shelf in your closet."

"I'm supposed to take fashion advice from an eight-year-old?" I laugh.

She drops her spoon and heads toward me with her hands planted firmly on her hips. "Trust me, Keats. It's your best look."

I don't know why, but I trust the kid. I plan on showering and putting on the suit when I get home.

"What color shirt?" I ask.

She purses her lips together. "Go with white. That way the tie will pop."

"Done." I lean forward to plant a kiss on the top of her head. "Learn something new today."

"You too." She smiles.

"Smart…as a whip," I quip.

She throws her head back in laughter. "Yes, I am."

Berk takes a step forward. "We'll talk more later?"

He's curious about Maren. I don't blame him. I haven't talked to my brother about a woman in a hell of a long time. "You bet."

"I want to meet Maren, " Stevie says as she marches back to her jar of oats. "I miss Dudley."

"I'll make that happen." I toss her a wave. "I think you'll like her."

Stevie scoops up a spoonful of her breakfast. "If you do, I know I will."

# CHAPTER TWENTY

*MAREN*

I SPENT most of today handling clerical duties for Keats. I saw him briefly this morning when he arrived at the office. I was hoping we'd get a few moments alone to talk about what happened last night, but Everett demanded a meeting with him.

That lasted almost an hour, and by then, it was time for Keats to head across town to speak with a scout who has been keeping tabs on two players on a high school basketball team.

As he was leaving, he stopped at my desk and promised that he'd be back early this afternoon.

It's quarter after three now, and if he doesn't stroll off that elevator soon, I'm going to send out a search party to find him. I've tried texting him twice and called once, but I've gotten no response from him.

I realize that he likely silenced his phone during his meeting, but part of me wonders if he's ignoring it because he's focused on something other than business.

I broke down mid-day and searched for my boss's name online.

I did that after spending over an hour learning everything I could about the Newman family. My time working at Knott Public Relations taught me that there's value in understanding the people you do business with.

There's no way I can know the Newmans well just by studying their social media accounts, but I think I have more insight into who they are than I did last night.

I have more insight into Keats too.

My online treasure hunt resulted in learning a few new things about my boss. He's been photographed at restaurants and clubs in Manhattan with some of his famous clients. In almost every picture, a different woman was hanging onto Keats.

In one of the images, a leggy brunette had her arms wrapped around his neck as they danced. In another, a blonde was straddled on his lap as he sat on a bench in a club. The image that caused me to close my computer's browser was of Keats on top of a bar kissing a woman with black hair as people around them raised their fists in the air.

Earl Newman had a point when he questioned Keats's reputation.

I turn to look when I hear the ding that signals the elevator's arrival. Relief washes over me when I realize that Keats is finally back.

He's dressed in the same dark blue suit and pink tie he had on when he left this morning. His clothing isn't wrinkled. His hair is still in place.

"Maren!" he calls out my name. "The countdown is on."

I stand as he approaches my desk. He stops mid-step as he takes in the pencil skirt and blouse I'm wearing.

Earlier, our brief exchange happened when I was seated,

so he didn't get the full impact of Arietta's fashion advice and makeup magic.

"Can I get a minute?" he asks with a perch of one brow.

I nod.

He waits for me to lead the way. I wonder for half of a second, whether that's because he wants to get a glimpse of my ass.

I shake my head trying to chase that away because we've already crossed so many lines that I'm dizzy with confusion.

Once he closes his office door, he rakes a hand through his hair. "The Newmans are set to arrive soon."

I almost make a comment about stating the obvious, but instead, I concur. "We don't have much time to get our stories straight. What are we going to tell them?"

His hand drops to his chin. "What do you mean?"

Did he completely forget what happened last night? The Newmans are under the impression that Keats and I share more than a boss and assistant connection. There has to be a way to explain that away without losing Fletcher as a potential client.

"Let's tell them we broke up last night," I spit out.

The corners of his lips curve up. "We're not telling them that."

I close my eyes briefly. "They think we're in a relationship, Keats. We're not."

"I know," he blurts out. "But you showed them another side of me."

I didn't. All I did was go along with the lie. If anything, that shows a side of me I don't want to exist.

I drop my hands to my hips. "What do you suggest we do?"

Keats's gaze follows my movements. He stares at my skirt. "We won't confirm or deny it today. They're coming to meet the team. We'll bring them in here for a quick hello, you'll say you have an important meeting to get to, and I'll take the reins from there."

Hypothetically, that could work, but the lie will still be in play. "When do you plan on telling them that I'm your assistant, and not your…"

"Lover?" Keats fills in the blank I left when my voice trails off. "I'll sign Fletcher and then down the road, I'll mention that we decided we're better as colleagues."

It can't be that easy.

"Maren," Keats whispers my name as he steps closer to me. "You did me a tremendous favor last night by not correcting Earl's assumption about us. It gave me a fighting chance. Without you there, the meeting would have ended before it started."

"I can't tell you how much I appreciate you giving me this job, Keats." I feel my skin heat. "But, I'm not sure I should have been at that meeting. My presence complicated things."

His arms cross over his chest. "I needed you there."

"Not really." I half-laugh. "I know virtually nothing about sports. I just started working for you, and my job description clearly states that I'm your executive assistant. The list of responsibilities on the contract I signed is all about tasks within this office."

A smile ghosts his mouth. "You didn't read the contract."

I'd take offense at that, but I can't because he's right. I skimmed it over quickly before I signed because I felt the building pressure of my parents breathing down my neck.

That's not exactly what happened. But my dad was trying to reach me the morning the contract was delivered. Once I got here, and spoke to Keats, I signed the contract in front of Everett after I gave the first two pages a glance.

"You attend social functions at my request." He brushes past me to head to his desk. "That includes dinner meetings, lunches, parties, and travel."

My stomach knots at that last word. "Travel? I have to go away with you?"

He glances at me as he places his phone and keys on his desk. "If need be."

"Where to?" I don't care where we'd go. I'm stuck on the fact that I agreed to all of this without realizing it.

Feelings can develop when people who work side-by-side spend time together outside of the office. It happened to me once and it didn't end well. I'm attracted to Keats, but he's my boss.

He straightens. "That's to be determined. We're staying in New York for the time being."

I exhale. "Good."

"You're not afraid of flying, are you?" He perks a brow.

I shake my head. "No."

A knock at the office door spins me around. "Should I get that?"

"Please," Keats says from behind me.

I take shaky steps to the door as I try to absorb the fact that my boss and I will be spending a lot more time together than I expected.

When I swing open the door, I'm greeted with a pair of arms wrapped in a pink cardigan. A woman with graying brown hair pulls me toward her. "You must be Maren. I'm Patrika Newman. It's so good to meet you two lovebirds."

# CHAPTER TWENTY-ONE

*Keats*

I STAND JUST out of reach of Patrika Newman's grabby hands. Maren is taking one for the team, and I'm grateful.

I wave a hand in greeting to Earl and his son even though they are thirty minutes early. I suspect that was planned. Earl strikes me as the type of man who does a hell of a lot of testing on those around him.

From where I'm standing, this unexpected early arrival couldn't have gone any better. I doubt Maren would agree since she's getting the life hugged out of her.

"Your office is cool, Keats," Fletcher says, looking around. "You can see the Empire State Building from here."

I glance toward the window. "It's a beautiful sight, isn't it?"

"You're a beautiful sight," Patrika Newman practically screams at me. "I knew you were hot as a griddle, but wow."

That's a compliment, so I smile. "It's good to meet you."

I wait for her to take a run at me, but she hangs onto Maren. "Earl told me that you all had the best time last night. I'm sorry I missed it."

Maren takes a step back, and by some miracle, Patrika loosens the death grip she has on her.

Earl finally steps into my office. "We're early, but we knew you wouldn't mind."

I flash a grin. "You're welcome here anytime."

Maren skims her hands down her sides to straighten her blouse. "Can I get anyone a beverage? We have coffee, green tea, an assortment of juices, and sodas."

*Like hell we do.*

The break room is stocked with coffee and some brand of tea that my first assistant loved. If anyone wants something else, there's water out of the tap and a bodega is a block from here.

"I'd love a green tea." Patrika grins from ear-to-ear. "You wouldn't happen to have honey, would you, honey?"

Maren laughs along at her joke. "We have honey."

*Since when and where the fuck did it come from?*

"If there's a bottle of orange juice, I'll take that," Earl says. "Fletcher, do you want a soda?"

"I've been craving one." He takes another look at the window.

"I'll grab those for you," Maren says before she shoots me a glance over her shoulder. "Anything for you, Keats?"

I shake my head because I'm too stunned to say anything.

She has to be the one who is responsible for this. Who knew assorted beverages could make people this happy?

I rarely meet clients here, so the extent of my offerings is slim. I'm glad she thought far enough ahead to anticipate this.

"I do have to leave shortly." Maren sighs, and

goddammit, even I believe her disappointment is legitimate. "I'm glad I had the chance to meet you, Patrika."

Patrika's lips fall into a frown. "Why are you leaving?"

"It's a work matter," I interject. "Maren is needed elsewhere."

"We need here her." Patrika tugs at Maren's arm. "I thought we'd have more time to get to know each other."

This isn't a goddamn blind date.

"Maybe another time," Maren says politely as she inches toward my office door.

Patrika glares at Earl. I know that look. I saw my mother direct it my father's way enough times when I was a kid. Patrika has an idea she thinks is brilliant, and she wants her husband on board.

Earl locks eyes with his wife and silently mouths something to her. I read every word that leaves his lips.

*Do you want them at our anniversary party? Go ahead. Invite them.*

I plaster on my best poker face because I'm about to land an invite to a family function. This isn't the first time this has happened. It's the third. I was invited to the wedding of the sister of a basketball player. He signed on with me a week later, and the tennis player who offered an invite to a birthday party agreed that I'd represent him before the night was over.

I fucking hope Finn Remsen won't be at this party.

"I'll be right back." Maren shares a smile with the room.

"Hurry back," Patrika calls after her. "I have a surprise waiting for you and your sweetheart."

Maren stops mid-step but then continues without a glance back.

This wasn't how I envisioned getting Fletcher Newman on my client list, but I do what needs to be done. If that means Maren and I have to play sweethearts in public, I'll do it.

I hope to hell, my assistant is up for it too.

---

MAREN COMES BACK to my office, carrying a tray with two tall glasses. One is filled with orange juice, and the other with a dark-colored soda. Next to them is a mug with a teabag string hanging over the rim. A small glass container marked honey sits beside that.

I don't recognize any of it. She put some serious effort into this, and I'm impressed.

Placing the tray down on the table that sits in the corner of my office, she turns to face all four of us. With a forced grin, she eyes me. "I should be going. I don't want to be late."

If she thinks she's getting out of here that easily, she's wrong. There's no way Patrika is going to let Maren exit my office without announcing her surprise.

"Give me just a moment." Patrika's index finger springs into the air. "I have an invitation I think you're going to like."

Maren's gaze lands on my face before she forces it back to Patrika. "An invitation?"

Patrika nods, causing a strand of her hair to fall from the bun on the top of her head. "We'd love it if you and Keats would join us to celebrate our twenty-fifth wedding anniversary a week from Saturday. It's going to be on the terrace at Howerton House."

Maren knots her hands together behind her back. I watch as she kneads her fingers. Not a sound comes out of her mouth.

I step in by clearing my throat. "We'll be there."

Maren's head drops. I know I should have told the

Newmans that we needed time to check our schedules, or we had plans but want a rain check. Both of those would open the door for Finn Remsen to steal Fletcher away from me.

"Earl will text you all the details." Patrika claps her hands together. "You're going to be the best looking couple next to us, of course."

"We can't wait," I say with a wide ass grin.

Maren taps a finger on the face of her watch. "I better run, so I'm not late."

Patrika goes in for another hug. This one is just as aggressive as the first. Earl looks like he's about to join in, so I take a step closer to the women. "I'll walk you out, Maren."

"What a fine man you are." Patrika wiggles her eyebrows. "We're going to have a mess of fun at the party."

Maren sighs. "It was lovely to see you all."

I'm on her heel the second she starts toward the door. I follow her silently to her desk as she opens the bottom drawer to grab her purse and phone.

By the time we're at the elevator, I'm wondering if I'll ever see her again, so I board it after her once the doors open on our floor.

As soon as they glide shut, she turns to me. "What are you doing? You can't just leave the Newmans like that."

I press the button to take us to the lobby. "They'll be fine."

She locks her gaze on the elevator doors. "Are we going to their anniversary party?"

Shoving both hands in the front pockets of my pants, I nod. "We are."

Still staring straight ahead, she whispers. "They think we're a couple, Keats. They're celebrating something very special, and we're deceiving them. It feels wrong."

"It's one evening. This could put me on the fast track to representing Fletcher."

"Once you sign him, we'll tell the Newmans we…"

I finish the sentence for her. "Broke up. I'll tell them you dumped me."

I watch as she cracks a smile. "We'll think of something to tell them."

"This isn't ideal, Maren." I lower my voice. "I know that. I fucking hate lying."

She turns to face me, just as the elevator reaches its destination. "That's a hundred dollars to the fund, Keats. They seem like nice people. I hope we're doing the right thing."

I motion for her to exit first as the doors open. "That party is another chance for me to show them that I'm the agent who will fight tooth and nail to get their son what he deserves."

She stays in place. "I know what it feels like to want something very badly. I know you want Fletcher as a client."

I want to know what she wants very badly. I'll get it for her. I'll get her ten of them if it makes her smile.

"I can help him build his career," I state without reservation. "He'll be in the right hands with me."

She reaches to press the button to hold the doors open. "Go back to the office, Keats. Don't keep them waiting."

I glance at the lobby to see Pace on the approach. "What the hell?"

"You swore, so that's a hundred dollars. I asked Pace to drop by to meet Fletcher face-to-face."

*Jesus.* This woman is incredible. I asked Pace to join us too, but he claimed he had plans he couldn't break. Fletcher is going to be over the moon when he sees his idol walk into my office.

"Maren!" Pace calls as he nears us. "I'm here just for you."

She motions for him to step into the elevator. "I can't thank you enough, but I need to leave."

The smile on his lips disappears. "Seriously? You're leaving me with this guy?"

"You two will be just fine." She steps off the lift. "Have fun."

We both stare after her as she walks away while the doors slide shut.

# CHAPTER TWENTY-TWO

*MAREN*

I SCOOT around Dudley as I head out of my bedroom. I'm showered and dressed for the day. I didn't put much effort into how I look this morning. I don't have the energy. I spent most of last night tossing and turning in my bed.

When I got home from work yesterday, Arietta wasn't here, so I paced the living room floor talking to myself until she opened the door.

Self pep talks are something my mom taught me. I'd catch her walking up and down the hallway in our penthouse when I was a child.

Sometimes she was trying to convince herself that she would pass over a piece of chocolate cake after dinner. Other times, I'd listen as she questioned whether she was a good mom.

I always stepped in when that happened. My mom devoted herself to me when I was growing up. She walked away from a promising career as a psychologist to stay home and care for me.

When I was twelve, she went back to work, and the light that had dimmed inside of her was bright again.

For years, she was always the person I'd go to for advice. That changed when she retired. I didn't want to burden her with my problems when she was finally settled into a calm place.

Bianca Marks is the person I look to for help now.

We met seven years ago at a yoga class. Bianca was cursing out a creep who was eyeing up the instructor. She chased the guy out of our class.

After that, we hung out a few times and built a friendship that has stood up to job changes, relationship disasters, and a few vacations together.

Arietta and I are close, but if something weighs heavy on my mind, I know Bianca will cut through the bullshit and give it to me straight.

I press the video call button on my phone, hoping I won't wake Bianca up. I crawled out of bed when I heard the apartment door shut as Arietta raced out of here before daybreak. Her boss must still be in Italy, barking out orders across the ocean.

I sit patiently waiting for the call to connect.

Bianca's messy brown hair comes into view. I can tell her head is resting on a pillow. One of her blue eyes cracks open.

"Hey, Bianca," I say quietly. "How are you?"

She shifts the phone to show the pristine state of the pillow and bedding next to her. "Alone."

I laugh aloud. "I'm glad I didn't interrupt anything."

Both of her eyes spring open. "I'm not. I wish there were something to interrupt."

She sits up far enough that the white silk bra she's wearing pops into view. "What's happening, Maren? Are you okay?"

"I'm fine," I reassure her with a nod of my head. "I started a new job a few days ago."

She rakes a hand through her long hair as she shifts her position again. "What happened at Knott?"

"Christian fired me." I sigh.

"He's a joke." She laughs as she places the phone down. "I'm going to grab a robe. Don't hang up."

"I won't," I call out as I watch her arm move across the screen.

"There," she says as she comes back into view with a light blue robe wrapped around her body. "Where are you working now?"

"Morgan Sports Management?"

"Keats Morgan is your boss?"

That surprises me enough that I suck in a breath. "You know him?"

She shakes her head. "I know of him. He's a pretty big deal."

*He seems to think so.*

"It's only been a couple of weeks since we talked." She tilts her head. "You landed on your feet quickly. I'm happy for you."

I know Bianca has to get to work, so I spit out what I called to say, "He's trying to land a new client. He's a big deal college baseball player."

"What's his name?" She rubs her hand over her eye.

"Fletcher Newman."

"He's going to kill it when he hits the majors."

My mouth falls open. "You know who he is?"

Nodding, she laughs. "I read an article online about him a

few months back. If I remember correctly it was all about up and comers in sports."

I inch toward why I really called. "His parents are celebrating their twenty-fifth anniversary and they invited Keats and I to the party."

She moves to the left slightly. "That's a good sign for your boss."

"It is, but there's a catch."

She tilts her chin up. "What's the catch?"

"They think we're dating." I sigh. "It started as a misunderstanding, but now we're caught up in it, so they think I'm attending as his girlfriend."

"Go."

I slump my shoulders. "I don't know if it's a good idea."

She leans closer to the screen. "Go, Maren. You like him, so go."

"I don't like him," I protest. "That's not it. I just don't feel right pretending we are dating."

She blinks twice. "You wouldn't have called me if you didn't like him. It's a party, Maren. Go and have fun. Don't overthink it."

"Is that what I'm doing?" I ask honestly. "Am I overthinking this?"

She skims a fingertip over her bottom lip. "Think of it as a work commitment. You go and do your job. If Keats makes a move on you that night, you find a bathroom and call me."

I let out a laugh. "I'm not calling you from a bathroom, Bianca."

"You might." She stands. "I need coffee. Do you want to meet for a cup before work?"

I glance at the time display on the corner of my screen. "I can't. I need to get to the office."

"We'll do it soon." She raises her hand to her mouth to blow me a kiss. "I love you, Mare. Call anytime."

"Love you," I whisper back before the screen goes dark.

## CHAPTER TWENTY-THREE

***K**EATS*

I SPENT the last hour listening to my niece tell me why dinosaurs are extinct. I learned that shit back in a grade I can't remember, but the fact is, Stevie's animated gestures and the expressions on her face made it a worthwhile lesson.

Berk dropped her at my place on his way to work.

He went in early to touch base with an author he wants to sign, so I made Stevie blueberry pancakes and bacon. I topped that off with orange juice served in a champagne glass.

Every other glass I own is crammed into my dishwasher. I finally remembered to press the start button on that before I left to walk Stevie to school.

I dropped her off five minutes ago, and now I'm standing across the street watching her with her friends. She's the chattiest of the bunch. That has everything to do with her mother.

Layna brought good things to this world. She cared for people who had less than her. She went to the animal shelter once a week to visit the dogs and cats with nowhere to go. She wrote poetry and short stories that my brother published before she died so she could hold her work in her hands.

Stevie represents the best of both of them.

I can only hope one day I'll have a child who will look up to her and learn about dinosaurs and everything else a kid needs to know to make it in this world.

I sigh when I feel my phone vibrate in the pocket of my suit jacket.

Stevie walked through my closet and chose my suit again today. I'm wearing a gray three-piece with a light blue shirt and tie. The shoes are black leather with red soles.

I may need to hire her as my stylist because I captured a few looks from both men and women on the walk here.

I read the text message that pops up on my screen.

**Pace:** *Get your ass to my place now, Morgan.*

Well, good fucking morning to you too, Callahan.

I type out a reasonable response because if Pace weren't killing it in the world of sports, he'd make it as a dramatic actor, and I won't feed into that.

**Keats:** *Keep typing. I don't see the word please on my screen.*

I look up to see Stevie filing into the school with her friends. The pink backpack slung over her shoulder sways with every skip of her feet.

My attention darts down when my phone vibrates again.

**Pace:** *My dick needs you.*

My brows pinch together as I read that once, and then again.

Pace and I play on the same team even though I've never worn a baseball uniform. I'm straight, and he's obsessed with chasing after women. That's clear by the number of calls my office has fielded from women looking for him after spending a night in his bed.

I type out a response.

**Keats:** *Come again and that's not a fucking pun, Pace.*

I stare at the screen.

**Pace:** *I sent a dick pic to a woman online and it's everywhere. I fucked up my contract, didn't I?*

I watch as the three dots bounce on the screen.

My fingers type out a message quickly.

**Keats:** *Don't send me the picture. PLEASE don't send it.*

**Pace:** *Help me out here.*

I turn to set off on foot to the nearest subway stop, typing as I go.

**Keats:** *I'm on my way. Don't respond to anyone, Pace. No one. Keep your mouth shut and your dick in your pants. I'll fix this.*

I will. This is a speed bump. I've helped other clients recover from worse. Pace will be just fine.

―――

"YOU'RE LOOKING AT IT, aren't you?" Pace swings open the door to his loft.

I keep my gaze pinned to my phone. "I'm looking at what?"

"My cock."

I grimace. "Hell, no."

He cants his head to catch a glimpse of my phone, but I shield it from his view.

I'm sneaking a peek at something I shouldn't, but it has nothing to do with what's in Pace's pants. I'm currently in Tribeca. Maren lives in this neighborhood, so I opened the map app on my phone to see exactly how far her apartment is from this place.

I might pull a teenager with a crush move and stroll past her building when I leave here. I don't expect her to be there, but I'll at least get a glimpse of the lobby.

"What am I going to do, Keats?"

I finally look up to see the naked chest of my client. He's wearing nothing but a pair of gray sweatpants. I dart my gaze up quickly because I don't want to be looking in the direction of his dick while I'm talking about it.

"You're going to do a charity calendar."

His eyes widen. "What?"

"You've seen them before." I brush past him to make my way inside his massive living room. "You'll pose nude with a baseball bat between your legs or a glove. Hell, I have no idea of that size of that thing, so maybe a baseball will suffice."

He grabs his crotch. "It's big, Keats. It's huge."

Shaking my head, I laugh. "I talked to the network on my way over here. They're on board for the calendar idea. They'll even let you push it on air. I'll call in some favors to get enough players for a year's worth of half-naked shots."

"That's going to fix this?" he questions.

I slap him on the shoulder. "You're going to need to say something on your socials. I'll help you craft that. We'll keep it light, and we'll weave an apology into it."

"And then I'll be good?" He perks a dark brow. "Everyone is going to know what my dick looks like."

"They'll forget about it as soon as someone more relevant drops a nude shot." I sigh. "Stop taking pictures of it, Pace. That's a big no from here on out. Understood?"

He nods. "Understood."

I point to where his phone is resting on his coffee table.

"Stay off that all day. I'll drop by later with a statement you can release."

"Okay." He nods. "Did Maren happen to see the picture?"

Shaking my head, I laugh. "If she did, she wouldn't be impressed."

He joins me with a chuckle. "I saw the way you looked at her in the elevator. You like her, don't you?"

I'm not diving into that gossip pool with him. I've worked hard to keep my personal life just out of reach of my client's curiosity. That blew up when Fletcher and his dad met Maren and decided she was my girlfriend. "Don't worry about that. Worry about what your mom's going to say when she realizes what you've done."

"Oh, shit." He hangs his head. "I need to figure out what I'll tell her."

"I'll help you with that too," I say, grateful that we got off the subject of my assistant. "I need to fix your fuck up, so I'm out of here."

"You're the man, Keats," he calls after me. "You're the best."

When Maren thinks that, I'll believe it. Until then, I'm doing what I can to be a better man every hour of every day.

# CHAPTER TWENTY-FOUR

***Maren***

*TALK about a hard day on the job.*

I laugh to myself as I glance toward Keats's office.

As soon as I got to work today, Myrie, one of the women who work in the legal department, brought up the Pace Callahan scandal.

Those are her words, not mine.

She flashed me a picture of an erect penis on her phone just as I was swallowing a mouthful of hot coffee.

I'm sure I scalded my tongue as I stood speechless and motionless.

I didn't want to see that.

Myrie did. After she showed me, her fingers slid over her phone's screen as she zoomed in.

*Why?*

I wanted to ask her that, but I can't judge what anyone else finds interesting. I'd rather see a man's penis in person than flashed all over the internet.

When Keats arrived to work, he was greeted with a round of applause.

I didn't join in because although he looked hot as hell in the gray suit he's wearing, it didn't deserve a standing ovation.

It took me a few minutes alone with Everett to realize that this isn't the first time Keats has had to deal with a situation like this. In fact, this is the third time the world has seen the cock of one of his clients.

I don't take nude selfies.

This is a reminder of why I never will.

Even though Pace's face wasn't in the picture, the woman who had the photo claims it's him.

She has a screenshot of a text exchange to back that up.

Pace may have an impressive cock, but he's not romantic. At least, he wasn't when he was sending out dick pics to a stranger. The gist of that exchange was that he was interested in hooking up and willing to share a preview.

"Maren!" Keats calls from where he's sitting behind his desk. "Do you have a minute?"

I have all the time in the world. I spent most of my day saying "no comment," to people calling Keats looking for a statement about Pace.

I've worked in public relations for years. I've dealt with scandals, including the exposure of extramarital affairs and political wrongdoing. I've never had to step into a situation like this.

I stand up and make my way to Keats's office. I don't close the door.

"Pace fucked up." Keats laughs. "How many people have called asking about his dick?"

He says the word so effortlessly that it sets me back a step. I skim my hand over the black pants I'm wearing so I can have a moment to catch my breath and chase away the blush I know has settled on my cheeks.

"A few," I say quietly. "I handled them."

"I knew you would." He pushes back to stand. "I'm going to take off for the rest of the day to deal with this. I'm heading over to Pace's loft."

I hold my breath, hoping he won't invite me to go with him. The last thing I want to do is sit in on a conversation focused on Pace Callahan's cock.

"How do you feel about the Newmans' party?" He asks in a low tone. "Our conversation from yesterday felt unfinished."

"Going to the anniversary party is important for work."

*That sounded robotic.*

Keats tilts his head. "It's very important for our business."

"Your business," I correct him.

A smile slides over his lips. "You still haven't read your contract, have you?"

Dammit. I meant to do that last night, but Arietta wanted to bake chocolate chip cookies, and I pulled clean up duties.

Arietta is many things, but a tidy baker isn't one of them. She used almost every bowl and measuring cup in our kitchen.

"I'm planning on doing that today."

"I'll save you the trouble." He rounds his desk. "Every employee receives a bonus if one of our clients signs a substantial deal."

"A bonus?"

He nods. "Fletcher Newman will be on the roster of a major league team in a few months. That's a given. If we convince him to sign with us, we'll all benefit from that."

I really should have read that contract through to the end.

This trip is way more important to me than I realized.

"If you're curious, the bonus is ten thousand."

I try to stop my smile with a bite to my bottom lip, but I fail. Keats sees it and smiles too.

"Let's do our part to get everyone that bonus." His gaze drops to the front of my red blouse before it shifts to my face. "Thanks for your help with the Callahan mess."

"I'm just doing my job."

"I'll see you tomorrow, Maren." He exhales. "Enjoy your evening."

"I will." I take a step back.

"Do you have plans?"

I'm taking Dudley to Donovan's vet clinic for a consultation about the microchip, so technically, that's a plan. "I do."

I watch his eyes narrow. "I hope a good time is had by all."

The tone of his voice makes my heart do a little flip in my chest. He's jealous. I hear it. I see it in the way his lips part, and his eyes widen.

"Goodnight, Keats."

He stays in place for a second, before he opens his mouth, only to slam it shut. A brisk nod is all I get before he's out the door and headed to the elevator.

# CHAPTER TWENTY-FIVE

***KEATS***

AT SOME POINT, I'll realize this is a hell of a bad idea. I'm not there yet, and that's why I'm standing on the corner, keeping an eye trained on the double glass doors of Maren's apartment building.

I hung out with Pace for a few hours after I left the office.

I ordered some food and sparkling water. Pace wanted beer, but alcohol and a phone with a camera, don't go together in his world.

He's blaming the dick pic on consuming too many tequila shots last night. I'm blaming it on his ego.

Both likely played a part.

After we wrote a statement that conveyed his genuine remorse for being so irresponsible, we posted it online. Then, we got to work rehearsing what he needed to say to his mother.

When he called her, all of our practice went to hell. She laughed it off and told him to keep it in his pants in the future.

He will. *I hope.*

The calendar shoot will take place later this month with Noah Foster at his studio. He's the best photographer in this city. He's shot nudes in the past. It was women years ago, but he agreed to take on the task of strategically hiding a dozen dicks behind sports equipment.

He's doing it for free, so I'll send a bottle of champagne to him and his wife as a thank you.

The proceeds from the calendar are going straight to an organization that funds research into prostate cancer. It seems fitting, given the circumstances.

Pace's father and my grandfather both succumbed to the disease, so this clusterfuck has turned itself around in the best way possible.

My phone buzzes in my jacket pocket, so I yank it out.

I glance at the screen.

**Berk: *Do u like pink unicorns or blue ones???!!!***

I scrub at my forehead. "What the fuck?"

I type out a response.

**Keats: *Where's your dad?***

**Berk: *Doing dishes!! I'm hiding!!!!***

I read that and then try to decipher the string of random emojis that follows.

**Keats: *Put the phone down, Stevie.***

My phone rings.

I laugh as I answer. "Your dad is not going to be happy."

"Ever?" she screams into the phone. "If he had someone to kiss, he'd be happy."

I close my eyes. I want him happy too. I don't know if a woman is the key to that or time.

"Where are you?" she questions. "I need to see Dudley."

"Need or want?" I glance at the front of Maren's building.

"Both," she screeches. "Bring him over."

"I will soon," I answer. "I'll talk to Maren and set something up."

"What color is her hair?"

I laugh. "Why?"

"Tell me."

"Red."

She squeals. "I want red hair."

"Stevie?" I hear Berk's voice bellowing in the distance. "Who are you talking to?"

"Keats," she yells into the phone. "He said I could have red hair."

I chuckle. "I didn't."

"You'll say yes if I ask," she retorts.

"No," I answer succinctly. "You're the most beautiful girl in the world exactly the way you are."

A tap on my shoulder turns me around in an instant. I come face-to-face with my assistant. Dudley is on a leash at her feet.

Maren's gaze narrows as she looks at my face. "I'm sorry to interrupt."

Disappointment or maybe frustration swims in Maren's eyes. She heard me. She fucking heard me tell Stevie she's beautiful, but she doesn't know I'm talking to my niece.

"I need to go," I say into the phone.

"I love you more than unicorns," Stevie whispers.

It catches my breath because I don't hear it that often. I bite my bottom lip before I reply, "I love you too, Stevie. Goodnight."

---

MAREN SMILES. "You were talking to your niece?"

Shoving my phone into the inner pocket of my jacket, I laugh. "She had a unicorn question."

She half-laughs. "Unicorn?"

"Do you like blue or pink unicorns?" I scrunch my nose feeling the familiar itch that comes whenever I'm within a foot of Dudley.

Maren must see it because she steps back two steps. "If I had to choose, I'd go with pink."

As hard as I try, I can't hold back a sneeze. "Me too."

"Bless you," she says softly. "I'm surprised to run into you here."

I can't tell if it's a genuine statement or a roundabout way of accusing me of stalking. I answer as if it's the former. "Pace lives a couple of blocks from here. I just left his place."

Maren glances at her building. "Is he doing all right?"

There's no concern woven into the question. I don't peg Pace as her type, but I have no real sense of what she finds attractive in a man.

"He'll survive," I chuckle. "Shit like this happens. There's always a way to recover."

"You swore." She points out as she looks at Dudley. "I should take him home."

"Have you had dinner?"

She drops her gaze. "I'm not dressed for going out."

Ripped, faded jeans, a white sweater, and a pair of sneakers are the perfect dinner attire, so I tell her as much. "You look amazing. We can share a pizza."

Hesitation sits in the air between us as she sucks in a deep breath. "I'm not sure."

I frame the invitation in a different way because I can't tell what's holding her back. "There's a big project coming up in a couple of weeks, and I could use your help. We should discuss that."

Talking about the charity calendar will happen tonight, but I want that to drift into a conversation about her. I want to know more about her.

I press my hand to the bottom of my nose as I feel a sneeze coming on.

"Let me take Dudley up to my roommate." She steps around me. "I'll be back in five minutes."

I sneeze one last time as I watch her hurry toward her building.

I've never looked forward to eating pizza with someone as much as I am right now.

## CHAPTER TWENTY-SIX

*MAREN*

I TELL myself that pizza with my boss is no big deal.

I ate a meal with Royce Knott once. Technically, I ate, and he talked. That business dinner started with him drinking two glasses of vodka as if they were ice-cold water on a sweltering summer afternoon.

As I picked at the crab cake I ordered, he talked about the woman who broke his heart. It was a brief glimpse behind the façade of the man I worked for.

The next day, I attempted to offer words of comfort, but he laughed it off, telling me that alcohol made him delusional.

We never spoke about it again, and that meal was the only time I saw him outside of office hours.

Keats is different. His personal life is forever cataloged in search results online.

"What kind of pizza do you like?" Keats asks the innocent question as we walk side-by-side toward a restaurant that Arietta recommended.

I tried to change my clothes into something more business-like, but Arietta bounced around in front of me, blocking me from going down the hallway to my bedroom. Dudley got in on the action, jumping up on her legs, causing her to giggle uncontrollably.

I was the one who fell on my ass when I kicked off my sneakers as I was putting on a pair of nude heels I had left in the foyer.

It was the light moment I needed to chase my anxiety away. By the time I got back down to the lobby where Keats was waiting for me, I felt more relaxed than I had when I spotted him on my way home from seeing Donovan.

"We should order a number fourteen," I say with a smile.

Keats glances at me as we pass a couple holding hands. "I'm in. You're the expert since I've never been to this place."

I haven't either, but Arietta has. She's told me to order the number fourteen just as I was getting on the elevator. I asked what was on it, but she told me to trust her. I do.

"I've never been either." I wave a hand to wave at one of my neighbors as he steps out of a barbershop with his cell phone next to his ear.

Keats waves at him too. "What do you mean you've never been?"

I gesture toward the right with a jerk of my thumb to signal that we'll be rounding the corner soon. "My roommate said this is the best pizza in Tribeca."

"You're putting a lot of trust in her or…him."

I hear the question woven into the statement. Keats is curious about who I live with. He must know that I'm not involved with my roommate. When we were at Nova, I let it slip that I don't have a boyfriend.

"Arietta is her name." I glance at him. "She's very trustworthy."

A grin perks the corners of his lips. "We all need someone like that in our lives."

I'm curious who that person is to him. Is it his brother? Maybe a close friend? Could it be his dad?

"How long have you known Arietta?" he pronounces her name carefully.

I keep in step beside him. "A year. I think she loves Dudley more than I do."

He lets out a laugh. "She's running even with Stevie then. She adores that dog. She's looking to see him soon."

That doesn't surprise me. Donovan is always telling me how many kids come into the vet clinic with their parents when the family pet is having a check-up. Animals can enrich a child's life. My dog, Bailey, did that for me. She was there to greet me whenever I got home from school, and she curled up next to me on my bed at night.

I cried for weeks when she died. I was twelve. My mom promised she'd get me a new pup, but I didn't want one. Bailey's place in my heart belonged just to her back then.

"Maybe we can set something up soon," he continues. "We can do it at my place. You can bring Dudley over, and we'll have dinner. You, me, Berk and Stevie."

"You're allergic," I point out, still unsure if meeting his family is the right move.

"I can manage a few hours with the furry monster." He laughs. "I'll pop an allergy pill or two."

I point as we near Frinzi's Pizza. "There's the place."

"So far, it looks like a good choice." Keats smirks. "People are waiting to get in."

I spot a familiar face in the line. Panic rushes through me. I admitted to Bianca that I like my boss. In less than two minutes, I'm going to be standing three feet away from her.

I steady myself with a deep breath. Bianca won't say anything. She's one of only a handful of people who knows my deepest secret.

As we get closer, I study her profile.

Bianca is beautiful. She's shorter than me. Her body is curvier. Her brown hair reaches past her shoulder. Her blue eyes are as bright as the sky on a sunny afternoon.

Today, she's wearing a black skirt and a light blue blouse. The black heels on her feet are higher than mine.

Just as we near her, she glances in our direction.

Her face lights up instantly.

"Maren!" she says my name with enough excitement to turn the head of everyone in the line. "It's you."

I rush to her, drawing my arms around her. "It's so good to see you."

As her hand pats the middle of my back, she lowers her voice to barely more than a whisper. "How are you?"

"Good," I reassure her. "I'm really good."

Still holding tightly to me, she whispers, "Are you on a date with your fake boyfriend?"

That sets me back a step. With a slight shake of my head, I smile. "It's a working dinner."

She jerks a thumb over her shoulder toward a man in jeans and a white button-down shirt. "It's a blind date for me. Kieran is his name."

I raise a hand to wave to the bearded blond-haired man.

"Hello." Keats moves to stand next to us. "I'm Keats Morgan. You must be someone important to Maren."

Offering her hand to him, Bianca tilts her head. "I'm Bianca. Maren is important to me too. Very important."

Keats smiles. He understands the message woven into her words. Bianca is as protective of me as I am of her.

He takes her hand and shakes it. "I'm her boss."

Bianca's blind date wanders over. "Hey, all. I'm Kieran Ratchford. Should we get a table for four?"

Bianca shoots him a look. "No."

Kieran's brow furrows. "Why not?"

I know the answer to that. Bianca wants me to have time alone with my boss. I see that in the way she's smiling at me.

"I changed my mind. I'm craving sushi," she says as she gazes up at Kieran. "That works for you, right?"

He grins, and with a wink, answers without an ounce of hesitation. "Whatever you want."

# CHAPTER TWENTY-SEVEN

***Keats***

IT'S BEEN a productive night so far. I've gotten a glimpse into Maren's personal life. I heard about Arietta, her roommate, and I had the pleasure of meeting Bianca. I didn't get an explanation for who she is to Maren, but I can tell the relationship is close.

Maren scrunches her nose as she looks at the paper menu that was placed in her hand once we were seated at a table in the corner.

Only one menu was offered. Maren grabbed ahold of it. I have no issue with a woman who knows what she wants, including what pizza she thinks the two of us should be dining on tonight.

"Number fourteen is a mystery pizza." She taps her finger to her chin. "Are you allergic to anything other than Dudley?"

I laugh. "Other dogs and cats."

Her face brightens with a smile. "I think we should trust

Arietta and go with the number fourteen. The food smells delicious, so it can't be a bad choice, right?"

I nod, even though I have no fucking idea what I'm agreeing to. I'm struck by how beautiful she looks with the small candle on the table between us illuminating her face.

I've met plenty of attractive women in my life, but Maren is different. She has a glow about her. Maybe it's from inner peace or pure happiness. Hell, I can't tell what it is, but I like it.

She orders the pizza and two bottles of domestic beer when the server revisits us to collect the menu.

"You like beer, don't you?" She smiles. "Did you want something else?"

*A kiss. Fuck, I want to kiss her.*

"I'm easy." I lean back on the wooden chair. "I eat whatever I can get my hands on."

Even in this dimly lit space, I can see that she's blushing.

I'd eat her all day and night if given a chance. My dick agrees. I shift on my seat to try and calm the bastard down.

I shouldn't be rocking a hard-on during our *business dinner*.

Maren picks at a fake arrangement of flowers in a tall vase sitting on the edge of the table. I pushed it aside as soon as I sat down so I could have a clear line of sight. I want to soak in the view all night. I could stare at her for hours.

"What did you want to talk about?" she quizzes.

*Marriage, kids, where she likes to vacation.*

I swipe a hand over my forehead. I need to fucking stop. Being this infatuated with my assistant is a red flag.

The server returns with two bottles of beer and a basket filled with breadsticks.

I snatch one to keep my mouth busy. This is the first time

I'm worried that my desire will outrun my brain and I'll blurt out something I shouldn't.

Maren watches as I chew. "Does it have to do with Pace and that picture?"

"His dick?" I ask as soon as I swallow.

She lets out a stuttered laugh. "Yes."

"What a fucked up mess that was." I shake my head.

"You swore," she points out. "You owe…"

"A hundred." I nod, taking another bite from the breadstick.

"I read the statement Pace posted to his Instagram account." She touches the edge of the basket with her fingernail but pulls back. "You wrote that, didn't you?"

I swallow the bread with a sip of beer. "How could you tell?"

"It was balanced." She rests her forearms on the table. "I think if Pace had been in charge, it would have been something like, *'You're lucky you saw my penis, but it won't happen again. Or it might.'* And he would have added the emoji with the tongue sticking out and an eggplant one too."

I huff out a laugh. "That's fucking hilarious, Maren."

She laughs too. "Have you read his posts? I lost count of how many eggplant emojis he's posted over the past few months?"

I laugh harder. "You've been stalking him?"

"Absolutely not." She hiccups her way through a laugh. "I looked at his account when I met him. It was for research only."

She drops her hand in the middle of the table when another hiccup falls from her. "Your hiccup cure. I need it."

It's not a fucking cure. It's a distraction. If I keep her talking, the hiccups will fade away. It's a trick my grandfather taught me a long time ago.

I don't tell her that as I cradle her hand in mine in the middle of the small table. I press my thumb into her palm.

She hiccups again. "You said fucking hilarious, so you owe another hundred."

It's worth it to see the satisfaction in her expression whenever she catches me cursing.

"Pace and a few other athletes I represent are going to do a photo shoot in a few weeks."

Sucking in a long, deep breath, she narrows her eyes. "That's related to his dick pic?"

Hearing her talking about a dick makes me hard. I wish we were discussing mine, but patience reaps the greatest rewards in life.

I press her palm harder. "The guys will pose nude with strategically placed sports gear. The proceeds will go to an organization doing great research work for prostate cancer."

The hiccups have vanished, but I hold tight to her hand.

She glances down. "That's a brilliant way to spin this situation. You thought of it, didn't you?"

Pride fills me. I've never worried whether a woman sees the best in me. I want Maren to know that there's more to me than meets the eye.

I nod. "If you can spin a screw up into something beneficial, do it."

She smiles in agreement. "I agree."

Her gaze drops to her palm. "My hiccups are gone."

I let go when I feel her tug her hand free of mine.

"Thank you, Keats."

*For what?* For holding her hand while I talked to her? I'm the one who should be thanking her.

I search her face looking for a clue into how she's feeling. She seems more relaxed than when she spotted Bianca outside the restaurant.

"What can I do to help with the photo shoot?" she asks quietly. "Do you need a photographer booked? Is there a place where you rent sports equipment, or will they bring their own? Should we get some robes for in between the shots, or are they fine to walk around nude?"

Forcing back a laugh, I smile. "I'll need your help scheduling session times for all the guys. We'll set up transportation to and from the studio for them. A few are flying to New York to do it, so we'll have to get flights and accommodations sorted."

She turns to where her purse is sitting on the table. With a slide of her hand inside, her phone appears.

Her lips move in silence as she repeats everything I just said. Her fingers fly over the screen of the phone. I assume to make notes of what needs to be done.

"I'll take care of all of this for you."

*I want to take care of you.* I open my mouth, wishing I had the goddamn courage to take the leap and say it.

I don't, because I sense if I tell her that I'm falling for her, I'll have her resignation in my hand within the hour.

She leans back when the server appears with two white plates and a large pizza.

I huff out a laugh when he places it on the table between us. He looks to me before his gaze settles on Maren. "Be careful. It's hot."

She only nods in response as her eyes widen at the sight in front of us. "What the hell is this?"

"It's a number fourteen," the server answers. "A grilled hot dog pizza."

# CHAPTER TWENTY-EIGHT

***MAREN***

THE LOOK on Keats's face says it all.

His phone rang once during dinner, and then again, just as he finished the last slice of the pizza.

I was reluctant to try it at first, so he said he'd dive in. He promised to give me his honest opinion.

I could tell by the smile on his face that he liked it, so I took a small bite.

Surprisingly, it was better than I imagined, but I won't order it again.

I still have no idea if Arietta genuinely likes hot dogs on her pizza, or if she was playing a joke on me.

I highly doubt it was the latter. Unlike my boss and me, I doubt my roommate could pull off a straight-faced lie if her life depended on it. I've been trying to bring up the Newmans' anniversary party all evening, but I haven't found a way to do that, and now I don't think I'll have the chance.

Keats lowered his voice when he took the call. Once he

said hello, and the person on the other end responded, Keats was on his feet, pacing a circle on the worn carpet near the entrance to the kitchen.

He's just out of my earshot, so I have no idea if it's a personal call or a business matter. Whatever it is, it looks like bad news.

Keats bobs his head up and down as he makes eye contact with me. There's no smile, just an acknowledgment that he knows I'm here waiting for him.

He pats our server on the shoulder as the young man passes him by.

It's those little things that tell you so much about a person. You can gauge the goodness that sits inside a person's soul by the way they treat others.

Once the call ends, he walks toward me. His eyes are downcast. Whatever that discussion was about, it didn't involve good news.

"I need to go," he says as soon as he's next to where I'm seated.

I watch as he pulls out his wallet and drops some bills on the table. It's triple the cost of the pizza and beers.

I push to stand. "Is it your niece? Or your brother? Is everyone okay?"

I know he has a sister. I have no idea if his parents are alive or in his life. Maybe this isn't related to his family. It could be about a friend or one of the athletes he represents.

"One of my clients was injured during training camp." He scrubs his hand over the back of his neck. "His family is in Germany, so I'm his go-to."

"Of course," I whisper. "Is it serious?"

"Serious enough to sideline him for a couple of months."

I move when he does. He steps to the left, so I round the

table. "I'll go to the hospital with you. I don't know him, but I'm great at food runs and sitting in waiting rooms."

Keats turns to me. Concern is set in his expression. "You'd do that?"

Without hesitation, I nod. "Let's go."

He drops his head. "He's in Philadelphia, Maren."

I should be relieved by that, but a wave of disappointment washes over me. This isn't a real dinner date, but I wanted more time. I would have taken it even if it meant pacing a hospital corridor by his side.

"Do you want me to make the travel arrangements while you pack?"

He glances at me. "That would help me tremendously. I don't know how long I'll be gone, so I want to swing by my brother's place to say goodbye to him and Stevie."

"I'll book the flight, a hotel, and arrange for a driver to pick you up at the airport," I recite my list aloud. "Is there anything else?"

"Let me walk you home."

It's already getting late for an eight-year-old. I'm sure his niece has a set bedtime, and I don't want to interfere with that.

"Why don't you go see Stevie?" I suggest. "The quicker you get there, the more time you'll have with her before she goes to sleep."

His gaze lingers on my face while silence sits between us. "That's the smart thing to do."

I nod in agreement. "You should get going."

He motions for me to lead the way out of the restaurant. "I'll write up a statement on the plane to release to the media. The team will too, but the more reassurance the fans have, the better."

Once we're on the sidewalk with the cooling evening air floating over us, I turn to him. "I hope he'll recover quickly."

"Me too." He shoves both of his hands in the front pocket of his pants. "Thanks for having dinner with me, Maren."

I'd tell him it was my pleasure, but the meaning feels too literal. Sitting across from him for an hour was fun. "I'll text you the travel details as soon as I book them."

"I'll be waiting to hear from you," he says as he turns to walk away.

I'll be waiting to see him again. I hope it's soon.

# CHAPTER TWENTY-NINE

*MAREN*

THE LAST FEW days have consisted of handling dozens of calls from the media and sponsors regarding Raymond Fischer's knee injury. With treatment and rehabilitation, the twenty-three-year-old will be back on the ice in a few months.

I recited that same line to everyone who called inquiring about him. Even though his team held a press conference the day after his surgery, people still wanted Keats to give them the inside scoop.

There wasn't anything to tell them beyond what was already in the press.

Keats is due to arrive back in Manhattan tomorrow.

He left Philadelphia as soon as Raymond's dad arrived. Keats called me to ask me to book him a flight to Orlando. A scout had a tip on a basketball player, so Keats decided to make a detour to meet with him.

Every call and text we've exchanged during the past six

days have been business related. It makes sense since I'm his assistant.

"Maren."

My head darts up when I hear my name. I'm surprised to see Fletcher Newman standing in front of my desk.

I push to stand. "Hey, Fletcher. How are you?"

I try to hide my shock. When I was going through the break room to see what I could find to serve the Newmans last week, Everett told me that unless they liked bitter coffee or old tea, they'd be unsatisfied.

He went on to say that Keats keeps the bare minimum of essentials on hand for the staff because clients never come to the office. That's why I went to a bodega nearby to stock up for the Newmans' visit. I've kept it stocked for the staff since.

"I'm good." He bounces in his sneakers. "Is Keats around?"

I glance toward his darkened office. "He's out of town. Is there anything I can do to help you?"

A spot of red appears on each of his cheeks. "It's kind of a guy thing."

I smile. "I guess I'm not equipped to help."

That draws a laugh from him. "I want to do something extra special for my folks. So, I think I'll rent a tux for the party, but it's in a couple of days. I thought Keats might know someone who could suit me up last minute."

I slide open the bottom drawer of my desk and grab my purse and phone. Then, I open the top drawer and reach for the company credit card Everett gave me when I signed my employment contract. I've only used it for the break room supplies. "I know a place. They'll have exactly what you need."

He glances down at the card in my hand. "That's not for the rental, is it? I have room on my credit card, I think."

Keats would want me to handle this. If he were here, his credit card would be in his hand too.

"I don't want you to worry about that." I point to the elevator. "All you need to think about is looking your best for the big night."

Fletcher sprints to the elevator to press the call button.

I follow as fast as my three-inch heels will allow me to.

As soon as we board the lift, Fletcher turns to me. "Keats is damn lucky to have you. I hope one day I'll find a girl as sweet as you."

*I'm his assistant. I'm his assistant.*

I silently chant that in my head as Fletcher smiles at me.

"Are you excited about the party?" I try and shift the subject to something other than my fake relationship with Keats.

"I'm more stoked for the beer that they'll have there." He laughs. "My dad expects me to eat clean. He wants me to exercise every day, sleep eight hours, and stay away from beer."

I study him as the elevator descends to the lobby. "What do you want, Fletcher?"

His brow furrows. "What do you mean?"

"Do you want those things too?"

He half-shrugs. "I guess. I get to drink two beers at the party, so I'm good."

The doors slide open, and with his hands in the front pockets of his jeans, and his shoulders tensed, he sets off to cross the lobby.

I fall in step beside him wondering if he's as happy inside as he looks on the outside when he smiles.

# CHAPTER THIRTY

***KEATS***

ALL WORK and no play make me a cranky as fuck.

I haven't gotten laid in a long time. It's been a hell of a long time. I had more than one chance this past week, but I kept my dick in my pants because it only craves one person.

Maren Weber.

That's right. I fucked my palm every single night while I imagined my assistant on her knees with my dick between her lips, or to change it up, I conjured up an image of her sitting on my face. To add to the mix, I envisioned fucking her from behind.

That's the roll call of fantasies currently running on a loop in my brain. Occasionally, I'll think about her spread-eagled on my desk while I slide my cock into her pussy nice and slow.

"Are you a pervert?"

*Jesus.* I hope to hell I'm in the middle of a drunken dream where I'm rocking a hard-on on an airplane while sitting next to a ninety-year-old woman with eyelashes that look like the legs of a tarantula.

"I asked you a question." The same high-pitched, gravelly voice creeps into my ear.

I crack open an eye and look at the seat next to me.

No dream. This is a fucking nightmare.

She circles one of her long red fingernails in the air before she points it down. "Your willy is wide awake, sonny boy."

I shut my eye again and shake my head. "Why are you looking down there?"

"It's that view or the clouds, so…"

I huff out a laugh. "I need a blanket."

"No." She leans closer until her breath gusts over my cheek. "You need a woman."

I open my eyes. "I'm Keats."

"Is that a name? Keats?"

"It's my name."

She rolls her big brown eyes. "What happened to John or Larry? I remember when almost every boy in school was named Walter."

"My brother is named Berk, and my sister is named Sinclair," I offer.

"Were your parents high when they chose those names?"

It's likely. When we were kids, our parents would send us to bed early and then go out on the balcony to smoke weed every Friday night. I didn't know that's what they did until a kid in high school offered me a blunt, and I recognized the smell.

"They're creative," I say. "What's your name?"

"Mary."

"Mary," I repeat. "Like Maren."

She rubs her nose. "No, like Mary. What's a Maren?"

I glance down at my watch. It's still over an hour until we

land at LaGuardia. "She's a woman."

She sets back in her seat to study me. "Is she the woman?"

I perk a brow. "The woman?"

"The woman who is responsible for that bulge in your pants." She glances down. "He went to sleep now."

I shake my head. "Maren is my assistant."

"You like her," she snaps back.

She's a stranger. What harm could come from telling her the truth? "I do like her."

"Does she like you, Keats?" She draws my name out slowly over her tongue. "Keats. So odd that it's a name."

"I think she does."

"With confidence like that, how could she not?" She shakes her head. "You're a good-looking guy, looks like you're packing a lot in your pants, and you smell good. You're a winner, so own it."

"I'm a winner?" I laugh.

"Look in a mirror." She pokes a finger into my shoulder. "Back in the day, I would have chased you."

"I consider that one of the greatest compliments I've ever received, Mary."

"Promise me, you won't let this girl slip away." She pats my hand. "Tell Maren that Mary says you're quite the catch."

"What about you?" I question. "You must have a Walter or two lining up to take you out?"

Running a hand over her short gray hair, she laughs. "A lady never tells."

The flight attendant approaches us. "Is there anything I can get for either of you?"

I shake my head. "I'm fine. Thank you."

Mary pipes up. "My friend Keats looks sleepy. He's going to need a blanket for his lap."

# CHAPTER THIRTY-ONE

*MAREN*

KEATS: *The plane just touched down. I'll make it.*

My ass drops onto the corner of my bed out of pure relief. I feel as though I've been holding my breath for hours.

Keats was delayed by a day in Orlando as he worked out a deal to represent his newest client. He promised me he'd be back in Manhattan in time for the Newmans' anniversary party tonight, but I was nervous.

I'm confident that I could have handled attending on my own, but I'm thankful that I won't have to.

I type out a quick response.

**Maren:** *Go home and get ready. I'll meet you at Howerton House.*

His reply is instant.

**Keats:** *Are you sure? I can pick you up.*

I'm touched by the offer, but it's out of his way. Howerton House is in mid-town. The venue features a garden terrace, a loft, and a ballroom. I've never been, but I'm excited to see it and Keats.

**Maren:** *I'm sure. See you soon.*

I take a second to stare at my screen before I hit send.

**Keats:** *See you there.*

"Please tell me that Keats texted you."

I look up to see Arietta standing in the doorway of my bedroom. I slide my phone into the pocket of the robe I'm wearing. "He's back in New York."

She moves across the floor with Dudley in her arms. She's been cradling him since we picked him up from Donovan's office yesterday afternoon. He implanted the microchip in Dudley and gave him a checkup and a bath.

Arietta commented that she liked the shampoo's peach fragrance, so he handed her a bottle and told her not to bathe him too often. I don't know how long she'll be able to resist that temptation.

"Thank goodness," she says. "It's makeup time, Maren."

I glance over to where the dress I bought a few days ago is hanging in my closet. It's black, sleek, and sexy. The fit is divine.

When I tried it on at the Ella Kara boutique, I was struck by the style. My back is completely on display, and the hem falls just above my knee. It's sophisticated but edgy enough to turn heads.

Arietta encouraged me to buy new shoes to go with it, but I'm relying on my favorite pair of black heels. They're comfortable, and I know I won't come home at the end of the night with blisters.

"Are you excited?" Arietta asks. "I'd be so excited to go to Howerton House. You'll take pictures for me, won't you?"

"I will." I nod.

She glances at my bouncing knees. "You're nervous."

I have to pretend to be Keats's girlfriend for the evening. I'm not convinced that I have the acting skills to pull that off. "I want everything to go well tonight."

"You mean you want Keats to get that Fletcher guy to sign on the dotted line."

Arietta has no idea that the Newmans think that Keats and I are involved. I didn't tell her because I'm hoping that after tonight, we can drop the lie.

"It will," she reassures me with a pat on my shoulder. "Stand up and stretch it out. It's time to get ready."

I push to my feet. "Are you staying home tonight?"

She places Dudley on the bed. "I'll hang out with my favorite guy."

"Mr. Calvetti is finally back from Italy?" I joke.

She laughs. "You know I meant Dudley, not Dominick."

"I know." I wrap an arm around her shoulder. "The bar down the street has half-priced martinis on Saturday nights."

Her eyes meet mine. "I'm good. It's the puppy and popcorn for me tonight."

It's a fake relationship with my boss for me tonight.

With any luck, this night will end with Fletcher Newman as a client. Once that happens I can go back to not being the pretend girlfriend of the man I have a real crush on.

---

I PRESS my finger to my phone's screen to cancel the Uber I ordered.

It was due to arrive ten minutes ago. I've been standing on the sidewalk outside my building anxiously waiting.

Ricky, the doorman, has come outside twice to check on

me. He disappeared when Mrs. Belars from 4B emerged from a car with an armload of packages. Ricky happily helped her with everything, promising me that he'd find a cab for me after he got back from her apartment.

I've lived in Manhattan my entire life. I know how to hail a taxi.

As one approaches, I lift my hand. I make eye contact with the driver. He smiles as he pulls up to the curb.

Just as I'm about to reach for the door handle, a hand darts out to grab it.

I turn to thank the person opening the door for me. A man with short-cropped blond hair scoots around me and slides onto the backseat.

"Are you kidding me?" I ask, with frustration laced into my tone. "This is my cab."

I don't have time for this bullshit. I'm going to be late for the party if I have to argue with this inconsiderate fool.

"It's mine," he says curtly. "I'm in a hurry, so kindly step away from the car."

"Get out of that car." The deep, velvet voice of a man sounds behind me. "Now, Hudson."

I turn to look at the man now standing next to me. He's tall with brown hair. He's dressed impeccably in a dark blue designer suit with a light blue tie. He's ridiculously handsome.

"No." Hudson crosses his arms over his chest. "Shut the door. I'm leaving."

The stranger leans into the car to speak to the driver. "Give us a minute."

The driver shrugs and then nods.

"Out." The suited stranger says. "Get out, Hudson."

"Or what?" The rude jerk shakes his head.

The stranger rests one hand on the roof of the taxi as he

talks to the jerk. "What the fuck is that? Are you five-years-old?"

I let out a laugh. I should be looking for another cab, but I want to see how this plays out.

"This cab is going nowhere other than this woman's destination." The handsome stranger smiles at me. "Give me a minute more, and you'll be on your way."

I nod silently.

Hudson finally drags himself out of the car. "I paid you once to help me, William. You don't get to call me out whenever you want."

William steps back to allow Hudson to move around me. "If you're acting like a selfish bastard, I sure as hell will call you out."

An obviously frustrated Hudson drags a hand over his head. "Where did you come from anyway? I didn't see you walking down the sidewalk before I got in the cab?"

"You were too busy thinking about yourself to notice anyone else." William picks a piece of lint off the shoulder of Hudson's sweater. "Apologize to this woman and offer to pay her fare."

"That's not necessary," I interject. "I'm fine paying for my fare."

"I have no doubt about that." William turns to me. "Hudson cost you valuable time, and he was a dick, so he's paying as a small way to make amends."

I glance at Hudson. He's nodding. "It's the right thing to do. I'm sorry, Miss. I got dumped yesterday and I love her, and I guess…"

"Save that for me." William pats him on the shoulder. "I'll buy you a drink at the bar on the corner. You can tell me all about it."

I smile at William. "Thank you."

As soon as Hudson has handed the cab driver a few bills, William offers his hand to help me get into the car. "I hope that wherever you're headed, you'll have the time of your life tonight."

I slide into the car, hoping for the same thing.

# CHAPTER THIRTY-TWO

***Keats***

I DROPPED my carry-on as soon as I got inside my townhouse. I raced to shave, shower, and put on a suit before I ran out the door.

I didn't even have time to stop by to see if Stevie approved of my outfit.

It's a dark gray suit, a light blue button-down shirt, and a tie with a dark blue diamond pattern. I look good. Mary would give it a big thumbs-up. I hope Maren does too.

I sprint around the corner on my way to the venue.

Howerton House is one of those landmarks that people flock to when they have a wedding, a milestone birthday, or they want to impress their friends. It's a centuries old building in midtown that's been converted into several event spaces.

I have no idea if the Newmans are looking to make anyone jealous tonight, but the garden terrace offers a full circle view of this majestic city.

I've been on that roof more times than I can count.

Tonight is the first time I've had goddamn butterflies in my stomach as I approach the building.

A jolt of something inside of me turns me to the left.

I stop in place when a cab drives by because I see her. I see the most beautiful woman in all of Manhattan sitting in the back seat.

Maren is peering out the window. Her gaze is locked on the building.

I'm not going to complain about that. If she were looking at me, I have no doubt that she'd see how fucking nervous I am.

That has nothing to do with Fletcher Newman, and everything to do with Maren.

I sprint the last half-block, so that I can pass the crawling taxi.

I make it just as the car pulls up to the curb.

The driver doesn't move, so I take a step forward and reach for the door handle. I swing it open.

Holy shit.

Fucking hell.

My thoughts alone should indebt me to the swearing fund by at least a few thousand dollars.

Goddammit, Maren Weber is beautiful. It's not just the dress, and her hair and makeup. Hell, all of that pales in comparison to her smile and that light that shines around her.

*Is this what goodness looks like? Is this my heaven on earth?*

"Keats," she says my name softly. "You're here."

I reach out a hand to help her exit the taxi. She does it carefully, keeping hold of the hem of the dress.

Once she's beside me, I reach for my wallet.

Her hand lands on mine again. "It's taken care of."

We stay in place like that, with our hands touching until

the driver clears his throat. "I'm hoping to get another fare tonight, folks."

"Sorry," I mutter as I bow down to wave at him. "Have a good night, sir."

"You too, bud." He smiles.

Slamming the door, I suck in a deep breath. I can do this. I need to do this. I want Fletcher on my roster, so tonight it's all about showing his parents that I'm the only man for the job.

I look at Maren. "Are you ready?"

Her eyes rake me from head-to-toe. "I'm as ready as I'll ever be, boss."

I point at the steps that lead up to the building before I offer her my arm. "I'm honored to be your date tonight, Maren."

She curls her hand around my bicep. "Let's get you a new client."

"Us," I remind her as we climb the stairs. "Let's get us a new client."

*Us.*

I could get used to the sound of that word.

# CHAPTER THIRTY-THREE

*Maren*

MY BREATH CATCHES as I survey the venue for the Newmans' anniversary party. The lights of Manhattan pale in comparison to the strings of white lights that hang from the wooden beams above the terrace.

Fragrant red and white flowers border the edge of the space, and a large three-tiered cake sits on a round table surrounded by framed pictures.

I take a step toward them, pulling Keats with me. I'm still holding tightly to his arm.

He reassured me as we rode the elevator up to the terrace that everything would be fine.

I'm starting to believe him.

Skimming my gaze over the pictures, I smile at what I see. There are two pictures of the Newmans at their wedding twenty-five-years ago. They're smiling brightly at the camera as they cut a cake similar to the one on the table. The other picture is of the two of them dancing.

Several photographs of Fletcher are there as well.

I sigh when I notice that he's dressed in a baseball uniform in every picture. In one, he's missing his two front teeth as he holds a small baseball bat at the ready. In another, braces cover all of his teeth. He's taller in that one. I'd guess he's ten or eleven years old. The last photo of him must have been taken recently. There's a determined look on his face as he stands with his hands on his hip, dressed in a baseball uniform with a cap slightly askew on his head.

Keats calls out when he sees Fletcher approaching us. "Hey, Fletcher. How are you?"

"Keats." He lifts a hand in greeting. "It's good to see you. Maren, you too. I can't thank you enough for this getup."

"You look fantastic." I round Keats to go to Fletcher. "They did a great job with the fit."

"Woah." Keats steps in place next to me. 'Tell me what I'm missing."

I give the floor to Fletcher because I can see he wants to say something.

"A couple of days ago, I was looking for you at your office." His gaze drops to the polished black shoes on his feet. "I thought it would be good to rent a tux for tonight. Maren took care of all of it. She even paid for it."

Keats looks at me. "She's amazing."

I can't hold back a smile. "I knew a guy who knew a guy."

Both men laugh.

Fletcher points his finger to the left. "My folks are here. It's time for a beer."

I glance at the bar. "Keats, you should join him."

Keats nods at me knowingly. "I'll bring you back a glass of wine."

"I'd like that." I turn back to Fletcher. "Enjoy that beer, Fletcher."

"You know I will." He chuckles. "I'll savor every last drop."

---

TWO HOURS LATER, I'm staring at the lights of midtown Manhattan. I've taken a handful of pictures and sent them to Arietta. When she texted me back to thank me, she told me the views look breathtaking.

They are. Not one is more impressive than Keats, though.

He's a beautiful man.

I feel him as he inches up next to me. "A hundred for your thoughts."

"That's a penny." I laugh.

"Your thoughts are worth more than anyone else's."

I almost reach up to grab my chest to stop my heart from beating so hard.

"Are you having fun?" he questions.

"I am," I admit.

We weren't seated near the Newmans during dinner, but we did get into a spirited discussion about baseball with one of Fletcher's uncles.

Keats did most of the talking, but I stepped in to shut the overly confident uncle down when I corrected him on the stats he was spewing out about his favorite player.

His eyes widened almost as large as Keats.

Since the other player is a client of my boss, I knew his record. I've spent a lot of time this past week studying our clients.

Our clients.

*Our.*

I like the sound of that.

"We should take a stab at some time with the happy couple." Keats gestures to where the Newmans are standing with two people.

"Let's give them a few more minutes to finish that conversation."

Keats nods. "That's extra time with our future client."

I glance over his shoulder to see Fletcher on the approach. "How did you know he was coming our way?"

"Intuition."

I look behind me and find a large mirror in a gold frame. "You're good."

Keats leans closer, dropping his voice to a low tone. "You have no fucking idea."

Desire pulses through me. It's not just from the words. It's from the proximity of his body to mine. I stare into his eyes, wanting to tell him that I need to know. I have to know what it's like to kiss him, to touch him. I want to be in his bed.

"You swore," I manage to say.

He perks a brow as his gaze drops to my lips.

"Keats." Fletcher slaps him on the shoulder. "Look at this view, man."

Keats keeps his eyes trained on my face. "I am. It's breathtaking, isn't it?"

# CHAPTER THIRTY-FOUR

***K**EATS*

I'VE NEVER WANTED anything more in my life than to kiss Maren Weber right now.

I'd trade a lifetime of deals with every elite athlete on the planet for a taste of her ruby red lips.

Her eyelids flutter shut as I breathe a path over her neck before I turn my attention to Fletcher because the kid's fingers are tap-dancing over my shoulder.

"Your folks are damn lucky to have a son like you." I lay the praise on thick because I want out of here and into Maren's bed.

Or my bed since that damn dog is living with her.

"Do you want kids?" He blurts out that million dollar question in front of a woman I want to have sex with.

Maren coughs.

I almost choke.

"My folks only had me," he goes on. "I think in ten or

twenty years when I'm ready to have a family, I'll opt for two."

"I'm an only child too," Maren pipes up. "It has its advantages."

Fletcher moves around me to get closer to her. "You don't have any siblings?"

She shakes her head. "Just me."

I stare at her profile as the curtain of red hair on her head moves when she talks. It's always curly. I fucking love that. It gives her a carefree look that makes me imagine her in a field of long green grass running toward me. I'd wrap my arms around her and spin her in the air before I lower her down and place a tender kiss on her lips.

*What the actual fuck am I daydreaming about?*

"Keats?" Fletcher shakes my shoulder. "What about you? Do you have siblings?"

I nod. "Sure."

I look to Maren to help me answer because all the blood in my body is rushing to my dick.

"Keats has a brother and a sister."

I thank her with a smile.

"What do they do?" Fletcher turns back to me. "Is your brother in sports?"

"He can't even bowl a strike to save his fucking life." I laugh.

Fletcher joins in, as does Maren before she offers a reminder. "That's another hundred dollars to the fund, Keats."

"You guys remind me of my folks." Fletcher looks out at the lights of Manhattan. "You're a solid team."

"That we are." Keats smiles at me. "That we are."

---

"SEE THAT BUILDING OVER THERE." Fletcher points a finger in the distance. "It has a hidden tunnel system beneath it."

Maren glances at him. "How do you know that?"

"Architecture is my porn." He chuckles. "I could spend days walking the streets of this city, staring at the buildings."

I catch the Newmans approaching in my periphery, so I turn toward them. Their son is the man I want on my roster, but these two call the shots, so it's time to turn on the fucking charm.

"Congratulations," I offer again for the second time.

"Keats." Patrika descends on me with her arms wide open.

I go in for a good old-fashioned mom hug. She doesn't disappoint.

"I can't thank you and Maren enough for the gift."

*Well, fuck.* Is that sarcasm spilling from her lips, or did Maren pull another rabbit out of her hat of brilliance and do something spectacular, again?

"The tea set is the most beautiful thing I have ever seen." Patrika pulls back, and I swear there are tears in the corners of her eyes. "It was just like the one we lost when we moved uptown."

Maren steps in to explain because a gift like that would never have been on my radar. Hell, no gift was on my radar. I dropped the ball on that. Thank fuck Maren was there to pick it up.

"I saw it at an antique store in Tribeca, and I thought you'd love it, Patrika." Maren smiles. "It had the silver design on the cups, so it seemed perfect for your silver wedding anniversary."

Patrika shifts on her feet until she's facing Maren. "I'll

treasure that forever. We've never received a more thoughtful gift."

*Home fucking run.*

Everything in this moment is perfect, from the way Fletcher is staring into the night sky, the joy in Patrika's expression, and the heart eyes Earl is shooting in my direction as he gazes at me.

I am going to represent Fletcher Newman.

I feel it, and it's all thanks to Maren.

# CHAPTER THIRTY-FIVE

*MAREN*

"I DON'T THINK there are enough words in the dictionary to thank you for what you've done, Maren," Keats says as we exit Howerton House.

"There are two." I laugh. "Thank you."

"Thank you," he repeats. "From the bottom of my grateful heart."

"You found nine words." I steady myself as we approach the steps to descend to the sidewalk.

"Can I take you home?"

I glance at him. I wondered if he would offer me an invitation to have a nightcap at his place, but I like that he's not making assumptions. I'm all for ending this night with a goodbye in front of my building.

I smile. "Sure."

Keats gestures toward the concrete steps. "Hold onto me."

I take a step toward him, but I'm stopped almost immediately. I let out a loud yelp as I feel my ankle twist in my shoe. "Ouch. Oh fuck. What the hell?"

Keats reaches his arm out to give me something to grab onto.

"If you were paying for swearing, you'd owe a fucking huge amount of cash."

I wince. "That's going to cost you."

He drops to one knee to get a better look at my foot. Patting his shoulder, he looks up. "Hold onto me, Maren. Take your weight off that ankle."

I do as I'm told even though people have gathered around us with their cell phones in hand. If they think they're about to witness a romantic marriage proposal, they're wrong.

"Well, well…" Keats stops to shake his head before he locks eyes with me again. "I've never seen this before."

I furrow my brow. "What is it? What's wrong?"

"Your heel broke off your shoe." He produces my broken heel in his palm. "I think you need a new pair."

"Dammit," I mutter under my breath. "These are so comfortable. They're my favorite shoes."

I attempt to step forward to remove my shoe, but the pain shoots me back a full step. I whimper.

"You twisted your ankle when your heel broke free." He moves to stand, edging his palm over my arm until we're holding hands. "You can't walk on that, Maren. You need to ice it."

I shake my head as I try and shake off the pain in my foot. "I'm fine."

To prove my point, I attempt to march forward on my uneven shoes. I stumble into his arms.

Before I know what's happening, he scoops me up and into his arms like I'm a bride.

I slap him on the shoulder. "Keats, put me down."

"You can't walk." His breath grazes over my cheek. "I'm going to carry you."

"To a cab?"

"My driver is waiting for us," he says as he starts in the direction of the steps.

"You're going to carry me down all those steps?"

He stops to look directly into my eyes. "I'd carry you down a thousand flights of steps if it meant you wouldn't be in pain."

Emotions I haven't felt before rush through me. I'm speechless. I stare at him. "Keats…"

"Let me do this for you, Maren," he says, oblivious to the people watching us as he starts to descend the steps.

Settling my arm over his shoulder, I reach down with my free hand to hold the bottom of my dress in place to cover my ass. "Thank you."

His lips curve up into a wicked smile. "You're welcome."

---

ONCE WE'RE in the lobby of my building and I'm settled on a cream-colored bench, Keats smiles at Ricky.

"I like that guy," he says to me.

I do too. I like everyone who works in this building. They've been good to me. This didn't feel like my home when my parents first handed me the keys, but I've come to love it here.

Keats reaches to move my foot into his lap.

I resist with a slap on his forearm. "You can go. I can make it upstairs on my own."

He didn't offer to carry me into the elevator. I think he felt my body tense up as he entered the lobby, and Ricky asked if he should call an ambulance.

I assured him that I didn't need that, so he directed Keats to set me down on this bench.

I know I can limp to the elevator and then again to my apartment door.

"I'd like to have a look." Keats raises a brow. "Humor me, Maren, and then I'll take off."

I give in and let him carefully cradle my sore foot in his palm. He rests it on his thighs. I tense again, but this time it's because this feels more intimate than when he was carrying me in his arms.

He tenderly touches my ankle. "How's the pain level on a scale of one to ten?"

"Four hundred and seventy-two?" I chuckle. "It really hurts."

He rubs it softly. "I'm going to pull off your shoe."

I nod. "Be careful."

He is. He slowly removes my broken shoe. His hands move gently over the swollen skin of my ankle. "You might have sprained it."

I sigh. "I'm ashamed to admit this has happened to me before. It will feel a lot better by morning."

He tilts his head. "Have many heels have you broken?"

"This is the third."

He rests my foot in his lap. "I hope I'm around the next time it happens."

I hope for that too. I hope he's around every time it happens.

"I should go up now." I point to the elevator. "Thank you for helping me, Keats."

He leans closer to me, his eyes gliding over my face. "Anytime, Maren."

I stay in that moment, soaking in how handsome he looks. There's a vulnerability in his eyes I haven't noticed before.

As he moves even closer, my body is drawn to him. We both lean in until our lips are mere inches apart.

His tongue skims over his bottom lip.

I watch the movement, mesmerized by how naturally sexy he is.

He tilts his head a touch. It's a silent invitation to kiss him. Just as I close my eyes, the sound of someone clearing their throat pulls us apart.

"Maren?" Arietta stands next to us with Dudley on a leash at her side. "What's wrong? Ricky called to tell me you were hurt."

Ricky stands a foot behind my roommate.

"I'm fine," I whisper, disappointed that the moment with Keats is lost.

Keats smiles at my roommate. "Hey, you must be Arietta."

"That's me," she affirms with a nod of her head.

"I'm Keats." His hand drops to my ankle. "Stellar recommendation on the pizza the other night. Thanks for that."

Her eyes travel over my face before they hone in on Keats. "You're welcome. What exactly happened to Maren?"

I notice the tremor in her hand as she grips Dudley's leash tightly. I reach out to touch her. "The heel of my shoe broke. I twisted my ankle. Keats carried me home."

She lets out a deep breath. "He carried you home?"

"Down a flight of stairs to his car and then inside to this bench." I grin.

With the slightest smile on her face, she looks at my boss. "Thank you for taking care of her."

"It was my pleasure," he says in a low tone.

I glance at him. He tilts his chin in my direction. "Rest well, Maren. Thank you for tonight."

I slide my foot from his lap and reach to Arietta for support as I stand. "Goodnight, Keats."

He rakes a hand through his hair. "If you need anything, call me."

I need him. I need to kiss and touch him, but I watch as he walks out of the lobby toward his waiting car and driver.

"Let's get you upstairs." Arietta wraps an arm around my waist. "Lean on me, Maren."

I do, but as we near the elevator, I take one last look over my shoulder, wishing that Arietta hadn't hurried to the lobby so that kiss with my boss would be a memory instead of a moment stolen away from us.

# CHAPTER THIRTY-SIX

*MAREN*

"I WISH Mr. Calvetti was more like your boss." Arietta places a plate of scrambled eggs and toast in my lap. "If I twisted my ankle, he'd tell me to suck it up, and then he'd want me to book him a table at Nova. His grandmother owns the best restaurant in the city. Why the hell does he eat dinner at Nova when he could be eating spaghetti with his grandma?"

I can't hold back a laugh.

My boss is a lot different than Arietta's.

Keats sent me a text message early this morning asking how my ankle was feeling. I responded quickly, telling him that it was much better and that I'd be at work on time tomorrow with flats on my feet.

He replied that he was heading home. He'd spent the night with another client. This time it's a hockey player who was arrested for being drunk in public. Keats went to see about bailing him out and then took the player home to his wife and kids.

I secretly hoped he'd bring up what happened in the lobby.

Maybe the almost kiss meant almost nothing to him.

It kept me awake.

I was close, but yet so far, to tasting my boss's lips last night.

"Are you daydreaming?" Arietta takes off her glasses, looks at the lenses, and then puts them back on.

"About how great this breakfast looks?" I quip. "Who wouldn't daydream about it?"

She sits down on the corner of the coffee table next to me. She adjusts the waistband of her red sweatpants. "I didn't get a chance to ask how dinner went. Did you have fun?"

I abbreviate the evening for her. "It was good. Keats thinks he'll sign Fletcher Newman to a contract soon."

She silently skims her fingertip over the logo on the front of the white T-shirt she's wearing. "Did I interrupt something in the lobby, Maren? I thought you two were talking, but I think you might have been leaning in to kiss him."

Innocence has always been wrapped around Arietta like a blanket. I know she has some experience with men. She admitted one night that she'd lost her virginity to her high school boyfriend before graduation.

There wasn't any fondness in her tone when she spoke of him, and when I asked how many men she'd slept with in college, she shut me down with the middle finger.

It was all in jest, but there was something about how she avoided the question that made me wonder if her past lovers are few.

"I think we were about to."

She jumps to her feet. "I fucked that up, didn't I?"

I can't help but laugh. "You didn't."

I don't want to blame her for my missed opportunity. Maybe it was fate's way of stepping in to wave a bright red warning flag. I kissed a co-worker once, and I not only lost my heart but my job too.

I'm not a proponent of believing that history always repeats itself. My last roommate couldn't pick up after herself, and she constantly left the apartment door unlocked whenever she left.

Maybe my luck is changing.

I couldn't ask for a better roommate than Arietta, and I doubt that I could find a boss I want to kiss as much as Keats.

"You should try and kiss him again tomorrow," she states with a grin.

I slide some eggs onto my fork. "As soon as I get to the office?"

"The early bird gets the first kiss."

"No." I shake my head. "The early bird gets the worm."

"Mr. Morgan is not a worm, Maren." She winks. "You'll know when the time is right."

I hope I will. My track record of reading the subtle nuances of men isn't that great. I thought my ex was about to propose the day he broke up with me.

"I'm taking Dudley for a walk. Text me if you want me to pick up anything."

I shake my head. "Thank you, but I'm good."

"And I can help you get into work tomorrow if you need me to." She tugs on her ponytail. "I can be a few minutes late."

"You're not worried that Mr. Calvetti will find out and get mad?"

Her hands fall to her hips. "What's the worst thing he can do?"

I swat my hand against my hip. "Spank you."

Her eyes widen before she lets out a giggle. "I'll be back in thirty minutes."

"I'll eat my breakfast." I tug on her hand. "You're the best, Arietta."

Her cheeks blush. "You stay on the couch and relax."

I raise my hand in the air as if I'm taking a solemn oath. "I promise I will."

She leans down to plant a kiss on my forehead. "See you in a bit. Have fun daydreaming about kissing Keats."

# CHAPTER THIRTY-SEVEN

***Keats***

I REST my head against the door of my townhouse. I've missed this place since I haven't been here for more than thirty minutes in the past week.

I had to rush to a police station in Brooklyn last night when one of my clients was arrested for being drunk in public.

His image can be repaired, but this reaches much deeper than that. He's been in a tailspin since his mom died last year. Vodka was his crutch until last night when he took a walk across the Brooklyn Bridge in tears.

The paparazzi wasted no time in uploading images and videos of his despair and arrest.

I called in a few favors to get an attorney on the case, and once bail was set, I handled that too.

We spent the next few hours talking about our plan forward with his wife while his kids slept. Hockey can wait. Rehab can't. He's headed to the best program in the state.

Grief counseling is a part of the healing process for him, and when he's ready, his teammates and his millions of fans will be ready to welcome him back.

Just as I'm about to plug my key into the lock on my door, it swings open.

I'm greeted with a scream from my niece. "Surprise!"

I shove my keys into my pocket so I can take her in my arms. She plants a kiss on my cheek. "I missed you, Keats."

Are there sweeter words than that?

Maybe hearing Maren say them would be even better.

I hold tightly to Stevie as I step over the threshold and into my home.

"You're strangling him, Stevie." Berk laughs from where he's standing.

I notice the paint spots on his jeans and T-shirt immediately. "What are you up to?"

"We painted the laundry room." Stevie jumps down. "Look at the paint on my shirt."

I glance down at the white splatter on the front of her pink T-shirt. "Daddy says this is what painters look like."

Wondering whether the paint is dry, I steal a look at my clothes. I'm dressed down in a navy blue sweater and jeans today. I had just enough time to fit in a quick shower before my phone rang last night with word of the arrest. I threw on the first things I could find in my closet.

I exhale when I notice my clothes are fine.

"I cooked bacon and made some heart-shaped pancakes." Berk jerks a thumb toward my kitchen. "I saved some in the oven. There's a smoothie in the fridge too."

I lean a shoulder against the doorjamb. "Thank you."

I don't have to ask why they're here. I noticed the date thirty minutes ago when I was on the subway platform. I called my brother to tell him I loved him. I left it at that. I didn't fear that I'd wake him up even though it's not even eight a.m. yet. I had no idea he took the call from my place.

Layna would have celebrated her birthday today. His townhouse is filled with memories that suffocate him on this day and the anniversary of her death.

My home is his refuge on those days. Keeping his hands busy is the solace he needs to escape his grief.

"We baked a cake for later." Stevie claps her hands together. "It's chocolate. That was mommy's favorite. Today is her birthday."

Sadness doesn't pepper her words. She remembers her mom fondly, but the grief she feels can't compare to what her dad experiences.

Stevie's comes in waves that roll over her less frequently now. My brother is still drowning. His daughter, his work, and his family and friends are his life preservers.

"I'm going to shower and change." I rake a hand through my hair. "It's been a long few days."

Stevie stands in front of me with an expectant look on her face. "Was your trip nice?"

Berk explained my absence to Stevie. He told her I had important work to get done.

"It was good." I straighten. "You'll be here when I come back down, won't you?"

She shuffles from one of her paint-stained pink socks to the other. "I'm not going home yet."

Usually, I'd play this game with her for as long as she wants, but I'm worn out. "Look in the front pocket of my carry-on."

Her smile brightens her entire face. "Why?"

We do this same song and dance every time I leave New York. "I might have picked you up something while I was away."

She dances in place before she drops to her knees. She slides open the zipper and yanks out a stuffed dog that bears a striking resemblance to Dudley.

"Keats!" She jumps back to her feet to wrap her arms around my waist. "I love him."

I pat the top of her head before I lean down to kiss it. "I love you."

"Me too." She squeezes me tighter. "Daddy and I love you very much."

That should be all I need in life. It has been for a long time, but I want more. I want Maren. I don't know if I can make that happen, but I'm going to do everything in my power to be the man she falls for.

# CHAPTER THIRTY-EIGHT

MAREN

I WALK into the office on Monday morning, steady on my feet.

I spent the better part of yesterday being coached back to health by Arietta. She got me off the couch at noon and into the kitchen. We made a salad together, and then once the food had settled, she guided me through some stretches and yoga poses.

It didn't seem like a lot of movement for my ankle, but it was tender by the end of the day.

It was a quiet Sunday, filled with lots of laughs with my roommate, good food, and thoughts of my boss.

As soon as I step off the elevator, I notice something on my desk.

It's a pink rectangular box with a white bow on it.

I glance around, but my co-workers are all busy tending to what needs to be done.

This is the first day I haven't arrived at the office before all of them. I took extra time to get ready this morning.

"Hey, Maren." Everett passes by me. "How was your weekend?"

"Good," I answer honestly. "How about you?"

"One of the best I've had in a long time." He smiles before he disappears down the corridor toward his office.

I stare at the pink box as I drop my purse into the bottom drawer of my desk.

It only takes a glance into Keats's darkened office for me to realize that he's not at work yet.

Scratching the side of my nose, I lower myself into my office chair.

That's when I notice a small white card next to the box with my name written on the front.

I open it and read the masculine handwriting.

*You said they were your favorite shoes. Keats.*

A smile creeps over my lips as I untie the bow and lift the box. I rip through the pink tissue paper and gasp. "What? How?"

I pick up one shoe. It's the same brand and size of the shoes I had on the other night. I reach for the other.

I don't know how Keats found another pair of the same shoes since I bought the originals when I was in college. It was at a small store in Boston that was going out of business.

My mom took me there for the weekend. She called it a girls' trip, but it was more of a rediscovery of our relationship. I had matured during my years in school, and she wanted to treat me to martinis and caviar.

I bought the shoes even though she insisted on paying for them. I wanted to show her that I was responsible and capable. Every time I slipped them on, I remembered that weekend.

I carefully place the shoes back in the box with shaking hands. "Wow," I say softly. "I can't believe this."

"Believe it."

I look up to see Keats standing in front of my desk. The smile on his face makes my heart swell.

"Thank you." I smile. "How did you find these shoes?"

"Anything is possible if you want it badly enough," he says. "Join me in my office, Maren."

I push back from the desk and stand on shaky feet. "Give me a minute?"

He nods and sets off toward his office door.

I watch as he walks away. The gray suit he has on may make him look sexy-as-hell, but the heart that beats inside his chest makes him irresistible.

I smooth my hand over the skirt of my dress. Sucking in a deep breath, I close my eyes and mouth to myself, "*It's okay to like your boss.*"

When I look toward his office, he's standing in the doorway staring at me. With a crook of his finger, he beckons me closer, and I go.

I let my heart take the lead.

# CHAPTER THIRTY-NINE

*Keats*

*IT'S okay to like your boss.*

Damn right it is.

I watched Maren silently say those words before she walked into my office.

She likes me. She fucking likes me.

Is it finally my turn to be the luckiest man on this planet?

"You look happy," Maren comments as she stands in front of me.

I close the door with a click.

Her eyes widen beneath long lashes. "Is something wrong?"

Everything is right. I keep that to myself and try and remember what I do for a living as I stare into her blue eyes.

"What is it?" She grimaces. "We can handle this together, Keats."

She's right. We can handle anything together.

I finally shake myself out of my infatuation fog and clear my throat. "Everything is fine."

She nods as she twists the end of the leather belt around her waist in her fingers. I glance down at the light green dress she's wearing. I would tell her she's beautiful, but I won't be able to stop there. How do you fully express to the most stunning woman in the world that she lights up every room she walks into?

"Are we going to talk about what happened the other night?" She lets out a breathy sigh. "We haven't had a chance to talk about that."

I take a step closer to her. "The almost kiss?"

Her eyes drop to my lips. "Yes."

"Arietta's timing is shit."

She bits her bottom lip to ward off a laugh. "You swore."

That draws me even closer to her. "I know, and here comes another. Do you agree that your roommate's timing is shit?"

She nods. Her gaze is still trained on my mouth, so I smile.

"Have you kissed anyone you work with before?" she asks.

"Everett," I answer. "Just once."

Her shoulders surge forward as she huffs out a laugh. "Are you serious?"

"I went to plant one on his cheek the day he became a grandfather." I tap my cheek with my index finger. "Everett moved, and the kiss landed on his lips."

Her head shakes. "Did this happen in front of everyone, or was it a private kiss?"

I lean in closer. "That one was public. This one will be private."

"This one?" Her eyes search mine.

"This one," I repeat before I cup the back of her neck, pull her to me, and press my lips to hers.

---

THE KISS IS SOFT. It lingers. I tug her into me, and she responds with the slightest sigh and a hint of a moan.

I dive deeper, tangling my hand in her hair as I skim my tongue over her bottom lip.

This has to be what a kiss is supposed to feel like because fuck me, I'm feeling things I've never felt before.

With a groan, I trail my fingers over her back.

"Keats."

What the fuck? My name has never sounded like that before.

I rest my forehead against hers to catch my breath, or to calm my heart down because that thing is slamming against the wall of my chest trying to escape.

"Maren," I say her name. "What the hell?"

She lets out the smallest laugh. "We kissed."

We did more than kiss. We connected on a level I never knew existed. If kissing her feels like this, what is fucking her like?

My dick hardens more when I think about touching her, bringing her to orgasm, hearing her come as she rides me.

"Kiss me again," I almost beg.

She takes a step back. "Is this wrong?"

"No," I blurt out without thinking. "How can this be wrong when it feels…"

"So good?" she interrupts me. "Did it feel good to you too?"

I glance down. "What do you think?"

Her hand pops up to cover her mouth when she gets an eyeful of the bulge in the front of my pants.

"I've never had a kiss quite like that," I confess.

"Me either." Her gaze drops to the floor. "I work for you."

I inch her chin up with a touch of my finger. "So?"

"That makes it complicated."

Shaking my head, I run my fingertip over her bare arm. "It doesn't have to be."

A knock at my door sends her back a step. "This is what I'm talking about. People will know what we're doing."

I don't give a fuck about that.

I stalk toward the door. "You'd think the closed door would be a hint to scram."

When I swing it open, I almost stumble back. "Stevie?"

My niece looks at me before her gaze darts to Maren. "Is that Maren? You kissed her, didn't you?"

How the hell did she figure that out in two seconds flat?

"You have lipstick on your mouth, Keats." Stevie marches into my office, holding tight to the stuffed dog I gave her yesterday. She stops when she's right in front of Maren. "I'm Stevie Morgan. I'm very happy to meet you."

# CHAPTER FORTY

*MAREN*

I STARE at the little girl in front of me with the big blue eyes. Her brown hair is braided to the side. She's sweet and incredibly polite.

I offer a hand to her. "It's nice to meet you. I'm Maren."

She slides her small hand into mine. "Keats told me you had red hair."

I smile. "He told me you love Dudley."

She cradles the stuffed animal in her arms. "This is Budley. He's my buddy when I can't see Dudley."

"Clever," Keats quips from behind her. "Did you drive here or what?"

She bends over in a belly laugh. "I'm eight. I can't drive."

"You're eight," he affirms with a nod. "Doesn't that mean you need to be in school right about now?"

"You're twenty-nine," she points out. "Doesn't that mean you should know how to brush your hair by now?"

I hold in a laugh.

Keats runs a hand through his hair. "What's wrong with my hair?"

"You need a cut." A man's voice calls from the open doorway.

"Daddy!" Stevie races over to him. "This is Maren. See her red hair. It's pretty, right?"

Keats's brother grabs hold of his daughter's hand and crosses the floor toward me. "I'm Berk."

I see the family resemblance almost immediately. Their hair and eye color are different, but Berk has the same strong features as his brother. He's slightly taller and nearly as handsome as Keats.

"Should I know why you're here?" Keats questions. "Am I missing something?"

Stevie glances at him. "I told you yesterday that I didn't have school today. My teachers are learning new stuff."

"It's a staff development day." Berk glances in my direction before he looks at his brother. "I took the day off, but Nicholas wants to meet up. I think it's good news. I was hoping you could watch Stevie for an hour or two?"

"Watch me watch him." Stevie points at her eyes before she levels her fingers at Keats.

He laughs. "Miss Morgan can work for me today."

That sets Stevie's back straighter as she stands tall. "I can work here?"

Berk nods. "Listen to Keats. I'll be back in a couple of hours to pick you up."

Stevie bounces in her shoes as her dad leans down to kiss her forehead. "Good luck, Daddy."

Berk tugs on her braid. "Thank you."

I smile when Berk looks at me. "It's been nice meeting you, Berk."

He winks at Keats before he turns his attention back to me. "I've enjoyed it too, Maren."

---

"DID you invite Maren to our concert?" Stevie asks from where she's sitting behind Keats's desk.

Keats took a seat in one of the visitor chairs facing his desk. I'm back at my desk, but with the door to Keats's office open, I can clearly hear the conversation between the two of them.

"You're ready for an audience?" Keats asks.

"As ready as I'll ever be," Stevie answers.

"Your confidence is next level." Keats glances back at me. "Why don't you grab some of that paper and make Maren a ticket for the concert?"

Stevie waves to me. "Do you think she can hear us?"

Keats looks back at her. "No. Why?"

"I think you should marry her, Keats." She sneaks another peek at me. "She's pretty and nice. You know that since you kissed her, and I like her."

"Let's worry about the concert for now," he expertly avoids her comments.

"Okay." She lets out an audible sigh. "Someone else might ask her to marry them, and then what?"

"If you get that ticket done in the next ten minutes, I'll ask Maren to take you to see Dudley."

I watch as she bounces to her feet. "Seriously?"

"Seriously?" Keats answers.

She drops back into the chair, grabs a piece of paper and a pen, and starts writing something down.

Keats stands and turns toward me.

I watch every step he takes as he approaches my desk.

When he's next to it, he looks down at me. "Did you hear all of that?"

I nod. "Every word."

He huffs out a laugh. "I don't know what it is about kids that age and marriage. They don't understand how complicated that is."

It doesn't have to be complicated.

I sit on those words as I watch him scrub the back of his neck with his hand.

"Can you take her to see Dudley for an hour?" He glances at the watch on his wrist. "I'm expecting a call from a scout in Denver."

"Of course, I'm happy to do that. I'm sure Dudley will be glad to see her."

"She's going to hand you a ticket to our concert." He shifts from one foot to another. "It's a piano recital, but feel free to say no."

I take a chance and ask the question sitting on the tip of my tongue. "Do you want me there, Keats?"

His eyes find mine, and I see the answer before he says anything. "I do."

"I'll RSVP as a definite yes," I say quietly. "I wouldn't miss it for anything."

# CHAPTER FORTY-ONE

*MAREN*

SPENDING an hour-and-a-half with an eight-year-old today was enlightening. I learned all about dinosaurs and unicorns.

By the time we left my apartment to head back to the office, Stevie was holding my hand and telling me about her piano recital tonight.

She has a special pink dress to wear. Keats is wearing something extra special too. She laughed when she told me that.

I'm watching her now as she hugs Keats and tells him goodbye.

She races over to my desk. "You'll be there tonight, right?"

I nod. "I'm excited to hear you play the piano."

"I'm pretty good for a beginner." She clutches Budley close to her chest. "My mom played it too, so I think she'd be proud of me."

Sadness nips at me. I never met her mom, but I sense she

must have been an incredible woman. Her daughter is remarkable.

"Try not to be late." She sighs. "I'm sometimes late getting up in the morning for school, and when it comes to doing my chores, I pretend to forget how to tell time."

She holds up her wrist to show me the face of the pink and white watch she's wearing. It flashes the time digitally. It's just after noon.

"Let's grab some lunch," Berk says.

"I'm in." Keats scoops up his phone off his desk. "How about you, Maren?"

I came to work today unsure of where things stood between Keats and me, and now a few hours later, we've kissed, and I've met some of his family.

I'll be seeing them again tonight, so I need to catch my breath.

"I have something to take care of, so I'll have to pass."

Keats brow furrows. He knows that whatever I have to do isn't related to work. "You're sure?"

I nod curtly. "Very sure."

"We'll see you tonight?" Berk asks as he reaches for Stevie's hand.

I keep my gaze on Keats. "I'll be there."

He smiles. "Good. I'll be back in a couple of hours, Maren."

"I'll be here," I say quietly as my gaze drops to the handwritten invitation on my desk.

As soon as they've boarded the elevator, I reach for my phone.

I scroll through the messages that were posted when I found Dudley. Some of the women included Keats's office address, but more than a few directed me to his home.

I compare that address to the one Stevie wrote down on the invitation.

*They match.*

Tonight I'm going to my boss's home. It's the place that he's taken many women to. I know I should be excited, but the pit of unease in my stomach is impossible to ignore.

Keats Morgan isn't a one-woman type of man.

I can't forget that. Not tonight; not ever.

---

I'VE LIVED in New York City my entire life, yet I've rarely ventured to the Upper West Side. It's like that with many people who call Manhattan home. We settle into our familiar corner of the city and find happiness there.

I stand on the sidewalk looking up at Keats's townhouse, wondering if it would ever be possible for me to find happiness here.

Maybe for a night, or two.

When Keats called after lunch to say that he wouldn't be back to the office today because he needed to see Pace, I jotted down the instructions he gave me for contacting several of the athletes who are going to appear in the charity calendar.

My job was simple.

I had to confirm their participation and then discuss what time frame worked best for them.

Three of the six men I called asked to speak to Keats directly. When I told them that he was unavailable, they wanted to leave messages.

All were the same, just worded differently.

Essentially, they wanted me to ask Keats if he would be

able to go to a bar or club with them the night of the photo shoot.

One said he wanted a celebratory drink at…and I quote, *"That rundown place in Lower Manhattan where we met Chelsey and Kelsey."*

Another mentioned a bar called The Tin Anchor where Keats drank body shots off a brunette.

I took down the messages and then cursed under my breath when I hung up the phone.

I can't expect anything from Keats but a good time.

I was worried about falling for him and trapping myself in the same situation I was six years ago when I dated Kollin Raiken, my supervisor at a radio station. He was two years older than me, handsome and charming.

I fell in love. He said he did too, but when things got complicated, I was dumped. The call from HR telling me I was fired came hours later.

I was dismissed from my job and his apartment on one of the worst days of my life.

Taking a deep breath, I climb the steps up to Keats's front door. I press the bell and hope that I'm not making another mistake.

## CHAPTER FORTY-TWO

*Keats*

YOU NEVER KNOW what is waiting around the corner for you.

Tonight, I'm dressed in my tuxedo, my niece is wearing a pink dress with a hem that skims the floor, and I'm about to open the door to a woman I'm falling hard and fast for.

I look down at the doorbell app on my phone to see the live stream of Maren standing on my stoop.

She's wearing a white dress that stops just below her knee. It's buttoned up the front with a lace collar.

She's clutching a bunch of fresh flowers in her hand. The stems are tied together with a pink ribbon.

I didn't think to give Stevie flowers tonight. I'm glad Maren did.

I want this night to be perfect for both my niece and Maren.

Stevie comes skipping towards me, wearing flat white

shoes. "I heard the doorbell. Are you going to open the door, Keats?"

Glancing over to where my brother is standing, I wink. "It seems that our special guest has arrived."

"It's Maren." Stevie jumps up and down in place. "She's our audience."

"What am I?" Berk shoves his hands into the front pockets of his black pants.

"The best daddy ever." Stevie blows him a kiss.

He does the same in return before he looks at me. "Get the door, Keats."

I do.

I walk across the floor and swing open the door.

A quiet sound escapes Maren as she takes me in. I slicked my hair back tonight, put on my best cologne, and tied my bowtie perfectly.

"You look great," she says quietly.

I smile. "You look better than great."

She fists the skirt of her dress. "The ticket said to wear a fancy dress, so I did."

"You sure did." Stevie peeks around me. "You look beautiful."

Maren takes a step forward, holding out the pink and white flowers in her hand. "You look like a princess. I brought you these."

"For me?" Stevie's voice quakes. "Really?"

Berk steps in place beside her. He strokes his hand over her hair. "That was very kind of you, Maren. Thank you."

"Yes." Stevie's head bounces up and down. "Thank you."

Maren sucks in a deep breath. "You're welcome."

"Come and sit." Stevie grabs hold of Maren's hand and yanks her forward. "I set up two chairs by the piano. One for daddy and one for you."

Maren glances back as she's pulled toward the living room.

"You're falling hard, Keats." Berk chuckles.

I don't argue. How the hell can I argue with the truth? I look at him. "She's different, Berk."

"I see it." He nods. "Stevie does too."

I turn to face him. "Maren is scared."

"Why?"

I shrug. "I don't know, but I sense it."

"If you like her, it's your job to find out why and then chase those fears away."

I can do that. I've chased my own fears away since I met Maren. Tonight, I start showing her that there's nothing for her to be afraid of when it comes to me.

---

MAREN AND BERK jump to their feet at the same time for a standing ovation.

Stevie beams in the adoration. She should. She hit every note on the mark. I've never heard *Mary Had a Little Lamb* played at that slow of a tempo, but dammit, it doesn't matter.

My star, and only, pupil made me proud.

"I did good?" She glances up at me. "Did I do it right?"

I pat the top of her head. "I couldn't have played it better myself."

Her smile tells me that she knows that's a fib. I've been playing the piano since second grade. I was forced to at first. Berk was too, but he switched over to the guitar.

Since Sinclair doesn't have a musical bone in her body, my parents insisted I stick with the piano. They didn't want their investment to go to waste.

It hasn't.

I kept up with the lessons, and when I bought this townhouse, my parents had the piano moved here as a housewarming gift.

Their granddaughter just belted out a tune tonight during her first private recital. I only wish they could have been here to see it.

My folks were bit by the same travel bug as my sister. They are currently RVing their way across the southern states.

By the time they drive back into Manhattan, they will have visited at least one city in every state.

Stevie yawns. "That was exhausting."

Berk, Maren, and I laugh in unison.

"It's time to go home to bed." Berk points at the flowers Maren brought. I put them in a vase I found in a kitchen cupboard before the recital started. "I'll carry that home if you carry Budley."

Stevie turns to me. "You're the best teacher."

"You make it easy. Do you know why?"

"Because I'm the best student?" She grins.

I drop to one knee to gather her into my arms. "You're the best student and the best niece anyone could have."

"Will we start on a new song tomorrow?" she asks as she messes up my hair with her fingers.

"I can't promise it will be tomorrow." I kiss her forehead lightly. "But it will be soon."

## CHAPTER FORTY-THREE

*MAREN*

I WATCH as Keats closes the door behind his brother and his niece.

Moments like this make me wish I had a sibling. I've often wondered if the bond between siblings is as strong as I imagine it to be. I'm close to Arietta and Bianca, but we didn't grow up together. We don't have the shared history that Keats has with his siblings.

Keats turns back to face me, tugging on the bowtie around his neck. "She did great, didn't she?"

I nod in agreement. "I thought it was perfect."

"Can I get you anything to drink?" He gestures down the hallway. "I have some wine in the fridge. If you want a cocktail, I can whip up something."

I smile. "I'm fine."

He rakes a hand through his hair, messing it. "You look beautiful tonight, Maren. I don't know if I told you that yet."

I could see it in his expression every time he glanced at me. "Thank you. You look great too."

"Better than the last time you saw me in this tux," he quips. "I'm sorry about that morning. I'm shocked you didn't quit."

"I am too," I joke.

"I know I'm not the easiest guy in the world to work for." He steps closer to me. "I've never had an assistant who felt like my partner before."

That's an unexpected compliment.

"It feels like I'm your partner?"

He takes a step closer to me. "Maybe I'm bullshitting myself, but from where I'm standing, you're as invested in signing Fletcher to a contract as I am."

"You swore," I say, following his lead and narrowing the distance between us with a step too. "I want you to sign him, Keats."

"Us." His gaze drops to my lips. "You want us to sign him."

I nod because I do want that. I want us to be *us*. I want it to go beyond a contract or a business deal.

Silently, he steps forward until we're mere inches apart.

"Maren." My name escapes him wrapped in a sigh.

Trying to calm down, I take a deep breath. I want to savor this moment because I know what's about to happen.

"I want you."

My eyes widen at the raw abandonment in his voice and fierce need in his eyes.

I see the want in him. I feel it in me.

"If I'm out of line, tell me," he groans out. "Tell me to go to hell and leave you the fuck alone."

I tell him, but it's not with words.

Instead, I lean forward, rest my palm against the center of his chest, and press my lips to his.

---

THE LIGHT from the hallway is enough that I can see Keats as he strips at the foot of his bed.

I'm still dressed.

He brought me up to his bedroom after we kissed.

As he rested his forehead against mine, he whispered that we'd only do what I'm comfortable with.

I want it all.

I want him.

I watch as he slides the shirt from his shoulders.

His chest is covered with a light dusting of dark hair. His body is as sculpted as I imagined it would be.

He drops his hands to his pants. I should look away, but I'm transfixed. His eyes haven't left me.

This might not be a slow striptease, but it's pushing me closer to the edge already. My hands are trailing over my stomach. The need in my core is so intense that I'm tempted to slide my hand into my lace panties and bring myself to orgasm.

I watch his chest move on a deep exhale when he pushes his pants, and then his boxer briefs down.

My gaze travels over his body, stopping to admire how hard he is already. I bite my lip to ward off the moan that's trying to escape.

He drops his hands on the bed. "Tell me you want me, Maren."

I nod.

"Tell me," he orders as he climbs on the bed.

His legs edge between mine. I feel the brush of his cock against my bare skin.

"I want you," I whisper.

He stops. "Say it again."

"I want you," I mewl. "So much."

His head dips, and I almost scream when I feel his lips skim over my thigh. "Spread your legs, beautiful. I want a taste."

With shaking knees, I do as he asks.

My hand drops to his hair when he licks a path over my hip. I edge my ass off the bed as he gently slides my panties down, and when his tongue touches my flesh, I let out a moan that is so deep and filled with raw need that he groans.

I come quickly and violently, jerking with the spasms of pleasure that roll through me.

"Keats," I call out his name as a plea for more.

*I want more.*

"Yes. Yes," he chants as he slides one finger into my slick channel. "That was only the beginning. I'll give you what you need. I'll give you everything."

# CHAPTER FORTY-FOUR

*MAREN*

KEATS UNDRESSES me with such tenderness that it almost brings a tear to my eye.

He kisses the skin he uncovers as he unbuttons the front of my dress before he gently tugs it over my head. When he unclasps the front of my bra, he presses his lips to the soft spot between my breasts, taking a moment to breathe in the scent of my skin.

"You smell like heaven," he whispers. "Heaven and home."

The solitary tear that's perched in the corner of my eye slides down my cheek. I chase it away with a brush of my hand.

I'm freefalling.

I thought I could control my heart, but that was a fool's wish.

My intimate experiences have never been like this. There

was always a rush to the main event, a sprint toward an orgasm.

Keats is different. He's taking his time and showing me that every second of this encounter is important to him.

I feel treasured in a way I never have before.

His lips run a path over my neck before they rest on my cheek. "I want to fuck you, Maren."

I turn toward him, resting my hand on his shoulder as I stare into his eyes. "I want that."

His gaze drops to my lips. "I've never met anyone like you. Your body is as beautiful as your soul."

Sliding my hand from his shoulder to the back of his head, I smile. "I have a beautiful soul?"

He nods. "You do."

"Tomorrow," I start on a stuttered breath.

"Tomorrow, nothing will change," he interrupts before he kisses me softly. "I'll still think you're the most incredible woman I've ever met."

I let my fears slide away as I stare into his vibrant green eyes.

He moves slightly, and I feel the plush crown of his cock brush against my hip.

I want him. I want this experience more than I've wanted anything, so I kiss him softly. "Get a condom, Keats."

His eyes widen. "Fuck."

"You swore." I press my body against his. "You owe a hundred more."

He tosses his head back in a chuckle. "I might as well write a check for ten grand right now because I'm going to lose it the second my cock slides into your sweet, tight pussy."

I drop my head. Desire pulses through me. "Keats."

He tips my chin up with his fingertip until our eyes meet. "I want you, Maren. I'll tell you every fucking chance I get."

"Show me," I say. "Show me, Keats."

———

WHEN HE PUSHES inside me for the first time, the grit in his voice sets my body in motion.

I curl around him. My hands dive into the thick, black hair on his head. My legs circle his big, muscular body.

He responds with another series of words that I can't comprehend. Words that are spoken out of need and sheer determination.

He's trying to keep it together.

The short pulses of his hips as he works to slide in drag me closer to the edge of an orgasm.

I can't come if he's not completely inside of me. I can't. I won't.

He's bigger than anyone I've ever been with. The fullness of his cock in my pussy is enough to steal my breath away.

He cups a hand under my ass. "You're so goddamn tight."

I open my mouth, but the only thing that spills out is a moan.

The next push fills me. The sound comes from him this time. It's a low-tone growl of approval.

"Fuck, Maren." He ups his tempo. "Shit. So good. So goddamn good."

He fucks me hard. Each thrust a testament to his need for me.

I cry out when his teeth find my nipple, and when I come, I crash into a wall of pleasure so intense that I lose myself. I lose all rational thought, and I scream his name over and over.

"So beautiful." He breathes the word over the skin of my neck as he fucks me slowly through my climax.

"Again, Maren," he bites out before I can catch my breath again. "I want another before I take mine."

The command is enough to send me straight into another orgasm as I writhe beneath him. He follows with a series of deep, slow thrusts before he comes with a toss of his head back and a hard groan.

## CHAPTER FORTY-FIVE

***KEATS***

I WOKE with a sore body and a full heart.

My bed was empty. I must have drifted off after I fucked Maren. I held her close as soon as I tied off the condom and tossed it in a waste can in the corner of my bedroom.

Her breathing leveled off as I ran my fingers through her hair.

I whispered that I was the luckiest son-of-a-bitch on the planet. In a sleepy voice, she reminded me that I was breaking the rules by swearing.

I broke every one of my goddamn rules last night when I took her to bed.

I promised myself I'd never fuck anyone I was falling for again.

The one and only time I let emotions lead me, I ended up alone in this townhouse wishing for a future that never transpired.

I swing my legs over the side of the bed and catch wind of the smell of coffee.

Maren must have wandered downstairs to put on a pot for us. I'll whip up some heart-shaped pancakes and then bring her up here for another round.

After I run my hand through my hair, I slide on a pair of sweatpants.

A thorough brush of my teeth follows a quick splash of cold water on my face.

I looked well-fucked and happy.

Jesus, do I look happy.

I smile at the lucky bastard in the mirror and silently remind him to pace himself. I may be feeling things for Maren that I've never felt before, but I can keep that to myself until the time is right.

I take the stairs two at a time as I race to kiss her.

That's my first task.

I'm going to pick her up, swing her in the air and then dip her down for a kiss, a slow, lingering kiss that will set her on fire.

"Good morning, beautiful," I sing as I sprint into the kitchen.

"Since when do you call me beautiful?"

My mouth falls open as I stare at my brother. "What the fuck are you doing here?"

My hand slams over my lips once I realize I swore.

I look around the kitchen for Stevie.

"She's at school," Berk says as he sips from a cup of coffee.

"School?" I question. "This early."

"It's almost nine."

My gaze shoots to the digital time displayed on the microwave on the counter. "Holy carp. I'm late."

"Carp?" Berk chuckles. "That's a saver. I'm stealing that one."

I cross the kitchen to pour myself a coffee. "Why are you even here?"

"Stevie and I saw Maren."

That turns me around to face him. "When?"

He takes a slow sip from his mug. The bastard is torturing me, and he knows it. The smirk on his face says it all.

"When?" I repeat.

"I was walking my daughter to school when we passed Maren." He lets out a sigh. "Stevie made a big deal about Maren's dress. She said she'd wear it every day too if she had a dress that beautiful."

I hang my head as I chuckle. "That sounds like our Stevie. How did Maren react?"

"She blushed." He smiles. "You're happy, Keats."

It's not a question. My brother knows me better than anyone. "I'm happier than I've ever been."

"I'm glad you're not letting the past play a hand in this."

It's the perfect opportunity for me to tell him to let his past go, but our heartbreaks don't measure equal.

He lost a woman he loved since they were kids.

I lost a woman I thought I loved for a couple of months.

Berk's wife died.

My ex-fiancée cheated on me.

You can't compare devastation to a distraction.

I got over Amber within a few months. My brother is still nursing a pain that I can't fathom.

"Maren is nothing like Amber," I say the words aloud that I've been carrying inside since I met the woman I spent last night with. "We're talking apples and oranges here."

"I know."

"You know? How?"

It's a rhetorical question, but in true Berk Morgan fashion, he answers it. "I've never seen you smile this much, Keats. She lights up your world."

I can't argue with any of that, so I don't.

I skip the coffee and instead go to my brother for a hug.

He stands and wraps his arms around me. "I'm happy for you, Keats."

I hope to hell one day in the future I can say the same to him.

## CHAPTER FORTY-SIX

*MAREN*

KEATS MORGAN IS a devil in a three-piece suit with a mouth made for sin.

I stare at him as he exits the elevator.

It's been over an hour since I left his townhouse. I didn't make it more than twenty feet down the sidewalk before I ran into his brother and niece.

My dress was the dead giveaway that I had spent the night with Keats. Stevie commented that she'd wear a dress like mine all the time if she had one, so I'm determined to find something similar to gift her with.

Maybe that's crossing a line, but it feels right.

Spending the night with Keats felt right too.

"You're smiling this morning, Miss Weber," Keats says as he approaches my desk. "A word in my office, please."

I nod as I feel the eyes of my co-workers on me.

I stand up. Smoothing my hand over the skirt of the navy blue shift dress I changed into, I walk into my boss's office.

"Shut the door," he says without turning to face me.

I click it closed quietly, taking an extra second to turn the lock.

"I left before you woke up," I point out the obvious. "I needed to get home to change before work."

He pivots to face me. His gaze travels over my body. "I want to strip you bare, Maren. I need to fuck you again."

My core aches with need. "Tonight."

"Tonight?" He edges a brow up. "That's a long time from now."

I take a measured step closer to him, fully aware that my nipples have furled into tight points. "You'll manage."

"Will I?" He drops his hand to the front of his navy blue pants. Cupping his erection through the fabric, he lowers his voice. "I'm as hard as nails."

"We're at work, Keats."

He stares into my eyes. "I won't touch you here, but as soon as the day is over, I want you on your knees in my bedroom."

The promise of that draws my tongue over my bottom lip. "Maybe I won't make it until the end of the day."

He steps closer until we're almost touching. "Don't lay a finger on that pussy before tonight. No pleasure without me, Maren."

I nod, hopelessly in lust with this man. "I won't."

His gaze trails over my body. "This conversation is going to kill me."

Huffing out a laugh, I lock eyes with him. "You'll live, Keats. I promise that the wait will be worth it."

---

THREE HOURS LATER, I'm still catching my breath from the conversation I had with Keats in his office.

I've spent the morning reaching out to several of Keats's New York based clients to set up dinner meetings with them.

My boss likes to keep the lines of communication open with his clients, and for him, that means face-to-face interactions.

I scheduled two lunches for next week and dinner with a client who asked me to thank Keats for the dollhouse he sent to his daughter for her birthday.

I'm responsible for that.

I saw the note in Keats's online calendar that he wanted to send a dollhouse to the girl, so I made the call myself to place the order so it would arrive in plenty of time for her sixth birthday party.

Glancing up when the elevator dings its arrival on our floor, I smile when I see Fletcher Newman exit.

He holds up a hand in greeting to me.

I glance at Keats's office and notice him on a call. His brow is furrowed, and his voice lowered as he speaks to a scout based in California.

I slide to my feet to intercept Fletcher.

"Hey, Fletcher." I step to the side to block entrance to my boss's office.

"Maren," he says my name with a bright smile. "I was in the neighborhood. I thought I'd stop by and say hi, so hi."

I let out a laugh. "Keats is on a call, but he won't be much longer."

He glances over my shoulder. "I came to see you."

I'm surprised, but I don't let it show. "What can I do for you?"

He produces a bunch of flowers from behind his back.

I gasp when I see the colorful mixture of roses, daffodils, and peonies.

"These are for you." He shoves the bouquet toward me. "My mom wanted me to get them to say thank you for the gift and for helping me with the tux."

I take them from him. "This wasn't necessary, but thank you, and please, tell your mom thank you too."

His gaze drops to the floor. "She said your heart is as big as Long Island."

I laugh. "That's big."

"She told me that good people do good things." He glances over my shoulder. "You're a really good person."

"She's an incredible person." Keats's voice sounds from behind me. "Maren is one in a trillion million."

Fletcher laughs. "Is that a real thing? A trillion million."

Keats steps in place beside me. "According to my niece, it is. Maren is special. You'll never find another woman on earth like her."

I glance at him but drop the gaze once I feel my heart race in my chest.

"I think my folks want to meet up with you two again soon." Fletcher draws both our attention back to him.

"Why don't the three of you come to my home for dinner one night?" Keats offers. "We'd love that, wouldn't we, Maren?"

*We.*

I'm beginning to love the sound of that word as much as I love the sound of us.

"We would," I say softly.

"I'll tell my mom to call you, Maren." Fletcher sighs. "I need to cut out now. I'm meeting up with someone."

"Thank you again." I raise the flowers to my nose. "I'm going to put these in water."

"I'll walk you out." Keats steps toward Fletcher but not before he skims a hand down my back.

It sends a shiver through me.

It's a promise of what awaits me tonight and, hopefully, for many nights to come.

## CHAPTER FORTY-SEVEN

***Keats***

THE HEAT of her breath gusts over my thighs.

I'm nude.

Maren isn't.

She ordered me to my bedroom as soon as she arrived at my townhouse.

I wanted to make things easy, so I was only wearing a towel when I answered the door.

Her dress hit the floor before her foot hit the first stair on her way up here.

Her bra was dropped somewhere in the hallway.

She's wearing red lace panties now. That's what I see as I gaze down from where I'm sitting on the edge of my bed.

I'm leaning back. My palms pressed against the bed coverings as she holds my cock in her hands.

"This is perfect," she says.

I huff out a laugh. "Damn right, it is."

She circles the tip of her tongue over the crown in a long, slow, meant-to-torture-me movement.

"Jesus," I spit out. "Please."

"You owe so much money." She tilts her head to give me a clear view of her tongue sweeping the length of my cock.

I drag my fingers through her hair, tugging it. "Suck my cock."

"You're impatient." She squirms her ass. "I want to take it slow."

"I want to fuck your sweet little mouth."

Her eyes widen. "Say that again, Keats."

I yank her hair to get her eyes on me. "I want to fuck your sweet little mouth."

Her lips envelop me before I can register what's happening.

I groan from the burst of pleasure that slides up my spine. "Fuck, yes."

She takes control. Her hand cups my balls as she glides her mouth over the length of me.

I drive my cock up and into her mouth, over and over again. I'm fueled more by the soft sounds of pleasure escaping her and the slickness of her tongue over my flesh.

I close my eyes and give in to all of it.

It's not just the driving need to orgasm.

It's the vulnerability and the feeling that I'm falling in love with this woman.

---

MAREN WALKS into my bedroom after a shower, wrapped in my navy blue bathrobe.

I almost drop to my knees from the sheer beauty of that.

This is the life I want. I want this to be my every day.

"We should eat," she says from the doorway.

I swipe the back of my hand over my lips. "I ate, but I'm ready again. Get on the bed. I want you on your knees this time."

I ate her after we fucked.

She told me she didn't think I could come again after the load I shot down her throat, but I'm always up for a challenge.

She laughs. "Don't make me laugh, or I might hiccup."

"I fucking love when you hiccup."

Her hands drop to her hips. "You swore, Keats."

"I'll write a check for a hundred grand this month." I scrub my hand over my chin. "That gives me room to curse a few more times."

She starts toward me. "I can order some food."

"Or I can cook for you," I offer.

Her eyes narrow. "You cook?"

Tugging on the belt of the robe, I pull her toward me. "I'm an excellent cook."

Her arms reach for my bare shoulders. Her eyes travel down my body, stopping at the waistband of my boxers. "What we did was incredible. I loved all of it."

*I love all of you.*

Fear stalls those words inside of me.

"I did too," I offer with a kiss on her lips. "You're amazing, Maren."

Her eyes search mine for something, but I can tell by the expression on her face that she doesn't find what she's looking for.

"What will you cook?" she questions with a purse of her lips.

"Hot dog pizza?"

She scrunches her nose. "What's the second choice?"

I huff out a laugh. "Who said there was a second choice?"

Her pointer finger lands in the middle of her freckled chest. "Me."

I stare at the sliver of skin exposed by the opening of the robe. I want to count those freckles and catalog them in my mind for eternity.

"Your second choice is leftovers."

She inches up on her heels to press a kiss to my jaw. "I love leftovers."

I grab hold of her chin to keep her in place. I stare into her eyes. "You like this, all wet and wild, makes me wonder how anything this beautiful can exist."

Her lips press together. "Wow."

"Wow, is right." I brush my lips over hers for a soft kiss. "You're the definition of wow."

I hold her there until she starts to pull away. "I should get dressed."

"No." I reach down to tighten the belt around her waist. "Wear my robe to dinner, and don't mess with your hair. I want you just like this when we eat."

"I won't change a thing," she reassures me. "I'll stay like this for as long as you want."

Forever.

I want her just like this forever.

# CHAPTER FORTY-EIGHT

*MAREN*

WHY DO moments this perfect have to be punctuated by bullshit?

That's a real question.

Whenever I feel my life is sailing along toward bliss, a hurricane creeps up and wipes out my happiness.

I stare down at the screen of my phone while Keats heats up pasta he ordered in for his brother and Stevie last night.

He said it's baked ravioli from Calvetti's.

It smells incredible.

The lump in my gut isn't from hunger. It's from the message that just popped up on my screen.

I reread it.

*Hey. I'm following up on Dudley. Were you able to reconnect him with Keats?*

I tap my finger over the screen of my phone.

"Maren?" Keats calls my name from where he's standing next to the microwave. "You look pissed. What's wrong?"

Was it that noticeable in my expression?

I drop my gaze back to my phone to reread the first message this woman sent to me weeks ago when I found Dudley.

*I met that dog when I stayed at his owner's place. Keats Morgan is the man you're looking for. He's a fun trip. Enjoy the ride!*

"It's nothing," I say.

Keats wipes his hands on a towel near the sink. "Tell me, Maren."

I don't want to ruin this perfect evening by bringing up one of his ex-lovers. "I said it's nothing, Keats."

He stalks toward me.

Even with a bare chest and boxers on, he's commanding. I can tell that he's not going to drop this, and I won't lie to him.

"Is your roommate all right?"

"It's nothing like that." I shake my head.

"What's it like?" he asks, ignoring the ring of the microwave signaling the food is warmed.

I struggle with how to tell him or whether I should. I could delete all of the messages and forget this ever happened.

But I don't.

"I got a message," I admit. "It was from one of the women who reached out to me after I found Dudley."

He leans his forearms on the island. "One of the women?"

The question is waiting to be answered, so I do it. "One of twenty-three women."

His gaze drops to the granite countertop. "Shit."

I look past his shoulder to the microwave. "Let's eat dinner."

His head shoots up. "No. We're going to talk about this."

I nod, unsure if I'm supposed to start this conversation or

not. My knowledge of his past lovers is limited to their names and the brief details provided on their Facebook profiles.

I only looked up a handful, and that was enough.

Pretty, successful, fun women responded to my posting.

Those same women have slept with the man I just got out of bed with.

"Do you want to see who responded?" I offer my phone to him.

Shaking his head, he raises his hand. "No."

I'm surprised by that. "Why not?"

"Those women helped me when I needed it," he says, keeping his gaze locked on mine. "None of them are a part of my life now. I was fucked after my fiancée cheated on me, so I screwed whoever wanted to screw me."

I'm stunned. I stare at him.

"I came home from a trip early and walked into the bedroom to find her riding the cock of one of my clients." He grimaces. "Talk about a fucked up mess."

"I'm sorry," I mutter.

"I'm not."

I look for more from him. We're so deep into this now that I want to know everything.

"Amber was wrong for me, Maren." He rakes a hand through his already messy hair. "I didn't realize how wrong until I met you."

"Until you met me?"

He rounds the island to stand in front of me. "After Layna died, I asked Amber to marry me because I felt lost, and she was there. We'd been dating for a couple of months at the time."

I nod.

"But, I realized pretty quickly that you can't chase grief away by ignoring it. You have to sit with it. You need to feel it. I thought planning a wedding would ease the pain, but it didn't."

I stare into his eyes.

"Even though I didn't love her the way I should have, I never cheated on her." He pats the countertop. "I stayed true to her, and when I found out, she didn't, I was tossed into a tailspin."

He glances over his shoulder when the microwave beeps again.

"I used sex to deal with all of it." He tilts his head back. "I didn't fully work through Layna's death, so random fucking buried the pain of that and the hit my ego took when Amber cheated."

"And now?" I question. "How are you now?"

"Honestly?"

"Honestly," I repeat.

"I've never been happier."

# CHAPTER FORTY-NINE

*KEATS*

I STAND in front of her, with all of my fucked up bullshit exposed, and my heart laid bare.

Until today, Berk was the only person who knew that Amber was unfaithful.

I told him the night I caught her cheating.

I went to a bar in midtown while she cleared her belongings out of my home. I drank to numb the pain, and then it turned into more.

I swallowed shot after shot to chase away everything.

By the time the bartender got my phone out of my hands and called my brother, I was falling over.

Berk arranged for Sinclair to stay at his place. Then he got in a cab and came to get me.

I cried on his shoulder.

I don't know what the fuck was wrong with me.

His wife died less than two months before that, but he

helped me up the stairs. He put me into the bed in the guestroom and promised he'd help me burn my bed.

That never happened.

Instead, he ordered me a new mattress, and on the day it arrived, I apologized for letting him down.

He hugged me and told me that I was lucky I found out about Amber when I did. He wanted me to know that my pain didn't matter any less than his. I needed to process the loss I was experiencing.

I shouldn't have done that by bringing a string of women home, but I did.

Sinclair was living here at the time. She stayed on the top floor and when she'd forget to close the door to the suite, Dudley wandered down the stairs and into the arms of the strangers I'd bring home.

Maren watches me as I eat my dinner.

She hasn't said anything since I confessed my sins. The only words out of her mouth were about the food and how good it is.

She places her fork on the island. Wiping a linen napkin over her lips, she turns to me.

"I loved a man once."

I close my eyes against the unexpected assault of emotions. Anger and sadness swirl inside of me. I swear I feel regret even though I didn't meet her until recently.

I would have given anything to be her first and only love.

"Who?" Curiosity drives the question from me.

"Kollin," she stops short of supplying his surname. "He was my supervisor."

"At Knott?"

With a shake of her head, she looks at me. "No, it was a long time ago."

Relief floods through me. I want this guy to be a distant memory, not my competition.

"I thought we would get married." She half-laughs. "I was young and stupid."

"What happened?"

A deep sigh escapes her. "Our future wasn't what he wanted anymore, so it ended."

I rest my fork on the plate in front of me. "Did you still want it?"

Her head snaps to the side. Her eyes lock on mine. "At the time, I did, but looking back, I realize it wasn't what I needed. He wasn't what I needed."

*I'm what you need. I will always be what you need.*

I swallow those words with a mouthful of wine.

"I've changed a lot since I was with him." Her hands fold onto her lap. "Isn't it funny how we envision our future at one point in our lives, but fate takes it in an entirely different direction?"

"I'm glad fate brought you to my office."

Her hand reaches out to cup my cheek. "I am too, Keats."

"We just chased all the skeletons out of our closets." I perk a brow. "I, for one, feel fucking relieved."

My phone rings.

I glance to where it's sitting on the counter. "Who the hell is that?"

The corners of Maren's lips edge up into a smile. "You won't know until you answer it."

"I'll ignore it." I gaze into her eyes. "They can wait."

It stops but starts up on a ring again almost immediately.

Maren tosses it some side-eye. "Our clients get into a lot of trouble. You should check."

I stare at her, feeling more connected to her than I've ever felt to another human being. "Our clients."

A blush covers her cheeks. "You call them that."

"Because they are our clients." I press a soft kiss to her mouth. "Just like we ate our dinner, and you're wearing our robe."

Her gaze drops to the front of the robe. "This is our robe?"

"I want it to be," I confess. "I want you to wear it whenever you're here. I want you to feel at home here."

She skims the pad of her thumb over my eyebrow. "We're moving fast, Keats."

We both glance at my phone when it starts ringing for the third time.

"Get the phone," she insists with another kiss to my mouth. "Business first and then pleasure."

"And then more pleasure after that?"

Her tongue darts over her bottom lip. "And more after that too."

I sprint to the phone and scoop it into my palm. Berk's name lights up the screen.

"What's the emergency?"

"What do unicorns eat?"

I laugh when I realize that it's Stevie on the other end of the call. I hear music in the distance. Classical music. That means my brother is working out.

I glance at the clock on the microwave.

"It's way past your bedtime," I point out.

"I was asleep, and then I woke up," she chirps.

"Where's your dad?"

"Lifting weights," she groans. "He has bigger muscles than the hulk."

If that's true, I need to up my game. Competition is a healthy part of my relationship with my brother.

"Put him on the phone, Stevie."

"Daddy!" she screams into the phone. "Keats wants to talk."

I watch Maren as she pours us each another glass of wine. I'm grateful that she's not rushing out of here. I want her beside me when I wake up.

"Hey." My brother's breathless voice takes over the conversation. "What's going on? What do you need?"

"Give Stevie a kiss and put her back to bed." I chuckle. "And don't lift too much. You don't want to hurt that old body of yours."

"Go to Hello Street, Keats."

*That's Berk code for go to hell.*

I reciprocate in kind. "Only if you go fork yourself."

Maren's eyes widen.

"Goodnight, little brother." He yawns. "You're a sweet fool."

That's not code for anything. That's what Berk said to me when I was a kid looking for the approval of the older brother he adored.

"I love you," I say it because I mean it.

"I love you too," he responds before he ends the call.

I silence my phone and set it on the counter. Maren is all I want to think about tonight. With the good grace of fate, this will be the beginning of a lifetime of nights to come.

# CHAPTER FIFTY

*MAREN*

WHEN I UNLOCK the door to my apartment, guilt hits me.

I spot Dudley immediately sitting in the middle of the floor.

Arietta is behind him with a mop in her hand.

"Hey," I say quietly.

"Hi, Maren." Her bright smile chases away some of my anxiety. "You look so good. Happy. That's what it is. You look happy."

I feel happy.

After spending the night with Keats, I rushed home to get ready for work. Arietta and Dudley were already gone, so I quickly showered, got dressed, and sent her a text message telling her I'd be home tonight.

It's later than I expected, though.

I went home with Keats for dinner, but we skipped food.

We ended up in his bed for more than two hours.

I'm hungry, sore, and very satisfied.

I crouch down to pet Dudley's head. "I'm sorry I haven't been around more to help with him."

Arietta drags the mop over the floor. "Don't be sorry. You're falling in love. There's nothing more important than that."

I stand up. "What?"

She rests the handle of the mop against the wall. When she turns to me, I see tears in her eyes. "I know you're falling in love with him, Maren."

I could argue with her, but there's no point.

It's as though she can see into my heart because I am falling for him. I may already be in love.

"I'm happy for you." She rushes toward me. "If he's good to you, I am so happy."

"He's good to me," I affirm with a brisk nod of my head. "We have so much fun together."

She scratches her brow. "More fun than you've ever had with a guy before?"

"Way more fun." I laugh. "It's on another scale."

She pulls me toward the couch with her hand. "Sit and tell me everything. Have you eaten yet?"

I shake my head. "No."

"I saved some salmon, wild rice, and broccoli I cooked." She sets off toward the kitchen. "You keep talking, and I'll get the food."

I don't know where to start, so I jump into the middle of it. "Our work relationship is amazing, and the other stuff is next level."

I watch as she places a white plate on the counter. "The sex is next level?"

I've never been shy talking about sex. "The best I've ever experienced."

She smiles as she plates my food from a dish that she pulled out of the oven. "You had an orgasm with him?"

The question takes me aback. I don't consider it too intimate to answer. I'm just shocked that she asked. "Many."

She picks up a napkin, and a knife and a fork before she scoops up the plate.

Once the plate in on my lap, she settles next to me. "What's that like?"

As famished as I am, I set the utensils on the plate and turn to her. "Have you never had an orgasm with a guy before?"

With a push of her glasses up her nose, she shakes her head. "No."

Sadness ripples through me. Until Keats, I didn't have the most considerate lovers, but they did make sure I was satisfied. With Keats, it goes beyond that. We connect in a way that enriches the pleasure.

"You need to experience that, Arietta."

"I want to." She nods. "I hope I will one day."

I place the plate on the table so I can gather her hands in mine. I look her in the eyes. "Sometimes, you have to chase after those experiences. I'm not saying you should hook up with a random guy, but if you start going out, you might meet someone."

Her hands tremble in mine. "You're right. I've been looking at a few dating apps."

I crack a wide grin. "I can help you weed through the profiles to find a guy who is perfect for you."

She tips her chin forward. "Someone as wonderful as Mr. Morgan?"

*Do other men like that exist?*

I keep that comment to myself. "If you're convinced that

Dominick isn't the man for you, you need to find someone who will see you as the gift you are."

"I want to be a gift to someone," she whispers.

"You will be."

Picking up the plate, she puts it back in my lap. "Eat, Maren. You need food and rest and maybe a bubble bath to soothe those aching muscles. I've heard great sex makes everything hurt."

"In the best way," I say before I dig into the food.

## CHAPTER FIFTY-ONE

***Keats***

WHEN I MADE the crucial choice of a career path, I never imagined I'd end up here. I'm in a studio with renowned photographer Noah Foster and a half a dozen dicks.

There are literally naked cocks everywhere.

Thank fuck Maren is back at the office arranging plans for our dinner tomorrow night with the Newmans.

"Keats." Pace stalks toward me completely nude.

I close my eyes. "Cover that."

"Covered," he calls out.

I crack open an eye to make sure I'm not being lied to. A well-placed football helmet shields his package.

I pity whoever owns that helmet.

"The guys stepped up to the plate for this." Pace smiles as he nears me. "I can't thank them enough, and you too."

I'm the afterthought, but I'm good with that.

The athletes are the stars of the show today. Truth be told, they are every single fucking day.

I won't complain because it's lined my pockets and set me up financially for the rest of my life.

I'm smart. I invest wisely.

"I didn't know she was coming." Pace lowers the helmet in front of him. "How do I look?"

I glance over my shoulder to see Maren on the approach.

"What the hell?" I mutter.

Her gaze is focused on my face and only my face. I reach out a hand to offer her comfort when she's a foot away from me.

"I tried to call you."

Those are the first words out of her mouth.

I yank my phone from my pocket. I tap a finger over the home button, but the screen stays black.

"It's dead." I close my eyes. "I forgot to plug it in last night."

"Hey, Maren," Pace says from where he's standing. "How are you?"

"Fine," Maren spits the word out. Her gaze is still locked on my face. "How are you?"

"I'm really, really good."

His cock is hard. He's rocking a fucking hard-on while he's talking to my girlfriend.

Girlfriend.

Is she my girlfriend?

"Keats!"

I turn when I hear my name bellowing from behind me.

Two of my clients, Colson Rees and Louie Holland, both raise their hands in greeting.

Louie's includes a lift of his middle finger in the air.

I take the high road and wave back. "Thanks for joining us, gentlemen."

Maren glances in their direction. I see the relief on her face when she realizes they're both dressed.

"Baseball players," she says under her breath. "They are baseball players, aren't they? Louie and Colson."

I smile at her. "You've been studying."

Her gaze darts back to the two players when Louie tugs the T-shirt he's wearing over his head.

Colson's hands drop to the button on the front of his jeans. "Do you want us naked now?"

He pushes his jeans down to reveal bright red boxer briefs.

Maren grabs my forearm. "Can we talk outside for a minute?"

*Gladly.*

I don't need the woman I'm falling head over heels for surrounded by naked dicks.

I take her hand and lead her past Colson and Louie grateful that in a room with this many men, she only has eyes for me.

---

WE STAND on the sidewalk in front of the studio as rain gently falls on us.

She inches closer to me. "I have an important message for you."

*I hope it's that she loves me.*

The words have been sitting on the tip of my tongue for days, but I haven't said them yet. I want to. Fuck, do I want to, but I don't want to scare her.

I stare into her blue eyes. "What is it?"

She perches on her tiptoes to drag her lips over mine. "Blue unicorns are the best."

I let out a laugh before I cup the back of her head and kiss her properly.

I let it linger as her breath stutters when I claim her bottom lip with a nip of my teeth.

"Stevie did call." She takes a step back. "But I came down to tell you that Finn Remsen wants a word with you."

"He wants a word?" I huff out a laugh. "Those are his exact words, aren't they?"

She nods. "He called and left that message an hour ago. He said he didn't appreciate you ignoring his calls, and it's urgent that he speak with you."

"He can wait." I kiss her again. "I have more important things to do."

"Wrangle cocks?"

Hearing her say the word makes me hard. "You're making me want things, Maren."

She inches closer, and with her lips pressed to my ear, she whispers. "Is one of those things me?"

I tug her closer. "Feel how hard I am."

She squirms against me as people pass by, oblivious to us. "Get back to work, boss."

I stare into her eyes. "How did I get this lucky? What did I do in my life to deserve this?"

"You're a good man." She rests her forehead against my cheek.

"You make me a better man." I close my eyes. "I want to be the best man I can for you."

"Keats!" Noah Foster's voice booms from the doorway of the studio. "You need to get inside. Let's get this thing moving."

I turn toward him. "Noah, this is Maren. She's my girlfriend."

Maren's eyes latch onto mine. A smile takes over her lips.

"Good to meet you, Maren." Noah bows his chin. "I need to steal your man for a few hours."

Maren grazes a kiss over my cheek before she turns her attention to Noah. "It's lovely to meet you too, Noah. Thank you for doing this for us."

*Us.*

Fuck, yes.

I want that to be one of her favorite words because it sure hits high on the list of mine right behind:

Maren.

Future.

Forever.

# CHAPTER FIFTY-TWO

***Keats***

I USED a phone charger that was plugged into the wall at the studio. Once my phone powered up, I was hit with a deluge of notifications.

Text messages from Berk ranged from one thanking me for connecting him with Nicholas Wolf to a few asking if seals have bad eyesight how do they keep their glasses on.

I'll wade through those later to separate the Stevie ones from the ones my brother sent.

He might be interested in marine life, but I'm betting Stevie is slowly getting over her fascination with unicorns.

I hone in on the text message Finn left me.

**Finn:** *Morgan, meet me today. You want to hear this.*

I didn't bother listening to the voicemails he left. They'll be more of the same.

Since the photo shoot is winding down, I type out a reply to Finn.

**Keats:** *What the fuck do you want?*

His reply is instant.

**Finn:** *Not your good looks and talent obviously since I have more of both.*

*Jerk.*

I respond the way I always do.

**Keats:** *Look in the mirror. You have ear hair and a chipped tooth.*

**Finn:** *Not anymore.*

I step out of the studio and onto the sidewalk. The experience I had in this spot hours ago was much better than this.

Kissing Maren in the middle of the day was what I needed.

I need more. I want more.

**Finn:** *You still there?*

I type out a message.

**Keats:** *Still impatient? Craving my attention as usual.*

I set off on foot toward the nearest subway stop. Finn can wait. I have to get to the office.

**Finn:** *It's about Vin Larchwood.*

Vin is a basketball player I've been trying to sign for the past two months. He's grabbed the interest of every sports agent in the country. I made it to his shortlist. Finn did too.

**Keats:** *What about him?*

**Finn:** *You're texting with his agent.*

"Fuck," I spit the word out as I stop to lean against a brick building.

This one hurts. I thought I had the upper hand.

**Finn:** *You're not going to congratulate me, Morgan?*

I'm bitter, and I'm pissed, but I'll give credit where it's due.

**Keats:** *Good on you.*

I've lost my fair share of potential clients to Finn in the past, but this one hurts.

**Finn:** *Word has it that we're the last two candidates the Newmans are considering. Prepare to lick another wound when I sign Fletcher.*

Word has it? What the fuck is that?

**Keats:** *Who the hell told you that?*

His response is instant and hits me square in the gut.

**Finn:** *Patrika did. I had dinner at their apartment last night.*

I rest my head against the brick and close my eyes. Goddammit. He's making strides with them. I need tomorrow night to be perfect. I have to seal this deal.

**Keats:** *May the best man win. We both know that's me.*

I descend the steps to the subway platform before his two-word reply hits my phone.

**Finn:** *It's on.*

———

"YOU WERE A LITTLE AGGRESSIVE." Maren licks her bottom lip. "I'm not complaining. I'm just saying."

She blew me just now.

I fed her dinner, carried her up the stairs to my bedroom caveman-style, and ordered her to get on her knees.

She happily agreed.

I thanked her with a string of expensive curse words. My dick showed its appreciation by coming down her throat.

My hands yanked on her hair. I tugged her closer and then held her in place while I fucked her mouth with long, slow strokes.

I'd blame it on my text exchange with Finn earlier, but it's not all that.

It was hot-as-hell watching her close her eyes and take my cock.

I tug her onto the bed with me.

She's only wearing a pair of pink panties and a smile.

"Give me a good three minutes, and I'll show you how much I liked that."

Slapping her hand over the center of my chest, she laughs. "Three minutes?"

"Two-and-a-half minutes now." I perk a brow. "Is that skepticism in your tone?"

She presses her lips to mine. "You can't possibly fuck me after that load you blew."

I glance down at my semi-hard cock. "I can."

Her lips trail over my jaw to my neck. She plants wet kisses there. "You're a world champion fucker."

I burst out laughing.

She does too. "I didn't mean it like that, Keats."

A hiccup falls from her lips before she tries to go on, "I meant…you're really good…*hiccup*…you're a great fuck."

"I'm a goddamn gold medal fucker." I pump my fist in the air.

Tears spring from her eyes as she laughs. "You're good in bed. That's what I meant."

Her eyes widen as she hiccups again.

She drops her hand in mine. "Fix it."

Still chuckling, I press my thumb into her palm. "I can do that."

She pushes closer to me. "You can do anything, Keats."

I'll do anything for her.

"Since we're taking a time-out from the best fucking in the world." She hiccups. "What did Finn want?"

I glance at her. "We're going to talk about work while you're almost nude?"

She pushes her chest out. "Ignore my tits and talk."

I lean down to take a nipple in my mouth. I bite it softly, luring a soft moan from her.

"Tell me, Keats." She rests her back on the sheet. "He was very impatient on the call I had with him."

"He signed a player I wanted." I kiss every one of her fingertips as I keep pressure on her palm. "He also told me that Newmans are down to two choices. It's him and us."

She darts up to a sitting position. "Seriously?"

I take her other nipple in my mouth and draw a slow circle around it with the tip of my tongue. "Seriously."

"I've arranged the perfect dinner party tomorrow, Keats." She presses her lips to my forehead. "I'm confident that once they spend one more evening with us, Fletcher will be a part of our roster."

I believe her.

She sighs. "My hiccups are gone, and it's way past three minutes, so?"

I watch as she slowly slides the panties down her legs.

Reaching behind me for a condom package, I close my eyes. Life doesn't get more perfect than this.

## CHAPTER FIFTY-THREE

*M*AREN

COFFEE with my two best friends is exactly what I need today.

Since Arietta and Bianca have never met, and both wanted some time with me, I thought this was the perfect solution.

We're at a crowded café in midtown.

Bianca chose this place because she knew she'd be in the neighborhood. Arietta agreed to show up after telling me that she banked so many hours that she was entitled to a little extra time away from the office today.

I'm the luckiest of the bunch.

So far, my day has consisted of speaking with the caterers and stopping by Wild Lilac. It's a floral shop owned by Athena Millett. She's engaged to Liam Wolf, who happens to be one of Keats's closest friends.

Athena knew who I was immediately. She made me feel at home.

While I sat and sipped a cup of tea she made for me, she arranged a gorgeous arrangement of white flowers for the centerpiece for our table tonight.

It was too large for me to carry to the townhouse, so she's having it delivered late this afternoon.

After this much-needed coffee date, I'm going home to shower, and then I'll head to Keats's place to get all the last-minute details in order.

He'll be waiting for me there since he's working from home today.

"You're beautiful, Arietta." Bianca gazes at my roommate. "Your bone structure is perfection."

Arietta smiles. "I can say the same about you, Bianca."

Bianca pats the top of Arietta's hand. "Maren tells me you work for Dominick Calvetti."

Arietta sighs. "It's true. Mr. Calvetti is my boss."

"My deepest sympathies." Bianca giggles. "He's a fucking tyrant."

Arietta laughs. "You know him."

It's not a question. It's a statement.

Bianca shakes her head. "I don't, but I've heard enough stories about him to understand that you are truly a saint."

Arietta takes a sip from the mug of green tea she ordered. "We should be talking about Maren's boss."

I inch up a brow. "We should?"

"You mean Maren's fake boyfriend." Bianca points a finger at me. "Who knew Maren had that in her?"

My roommate's brow furrows. "Fake boyfriend? What do you mean?"

*Dammit.*

I never told Arietta about that because things shifted so quickly between Keats and me.

Bianca tosses me a look meant to convey her regret for bringing it up, but I chase that away with a soft smile.

"Remember that night I went to Nova with Keats for a business dinner?"

Arietta nods. "You went to meet a baseball player."

"Fletcher Newman," Bianca clarifies.

"When he walked into the restaurant with his dad, Keats was holding my hand and telling me that he wanted me to meet his brother and his niece."

Arietta pushes her finger against the frame of her glasses. "Oh, boy."

I nod. "They assumed we were dating, but Keats was trying to stop my hiccups and the invite to meet his family was something he said he did with all of his assistants. It was completely innocent..."

"But it didn't look that way," Bianca interjects.

I shake my head. "No. It looked like we were a couple, and from there, it just took off. The Newmans saw us as a strong team inside and outside of the office, so we went with it."

Arietta scratches her chin. "Did they think you were a couple when you went to their anniversary party?"

I nod. "They did. They assumed we were together."

Arietta drops her gaze to the mug in front of her. I don't want her to feel disappointed in me. "I'm sorry I didn't tell you, Arietta."

She glances up. "Don't be sorry. Everyone has secrets they don't always share."

"We're good?" I ask, hopeful that this won't change anything between us.

"We're good," she reassures me with a pat of her hand on my forearm. "Drink up, ladies. I need to go back to work soon."

I TOOK my time in the shower. It was both relaxing and invigorating. Now that I know that the Newmans have narrowed the field of potential agents to two, I'm more determined than ever to get Keats that contract.

I run a brush through my hair.

I've always had curly hair. I despised it when I was a teenager, but as I got older, I started to embrace it.

I love it now.

After applying moisturizer to my face, I set my ass down on the corner of my bed.

When I reach for my phone, I'm surprised to see a missed called from Royce Knott.

I debate whether or not I should listen to the voicemail message. I'm happy working with Keats. It feels as though we're building a strong team. I may not be chasing my dream of a career in public relations, but this is the next best thing.

All of my experience and insight is helping me be the best assistant I can to Keats.

I finally tap the voicemail message icon to listen.

"Maren? Jesus. I am so sorry about what happened to you. I need to see you. Name the time and place. I want to make this right."

The message ends with me staring at my phone.

I play it again.

The voice belongs to Royce Knott, but I've never heard compassion in his tone before.

I don't like leaving anything unfinished, so I press the button to call his number.

# CHAPTER FIFTY-FOUR

***K**EATS*

ONE MOMENT the world can be in the palm of your hand, and the next second, it can turn around and slap you across the face leaving you senseless.

That's what I feel now.

I'm staring into a diner looking at the woman I love in the arms of another man. I saw a flash of red hair as I turned the corner. I knew it was Maren. That shot of need inside of me told me that. I tried to catch up, but she disappeared into the diner before I could reach her.

I don't know who the fuck the guy is that Maren is hugging.

She's supposed to be at my townhouse getting ready for the dinner tonight. Instead, she's clutching onto a tall guy with blond hair who looks like he wants to make her every dream come true.

I know regret when I see it on a man's face.

It's there on mine when I wake up every morning.

I used women for years to bury my feelings. I didn't care enough about them to remember their names or what they liked in bed.

When they called the next day, I'd answer with an excuse about being busy.

I was a coward.

I'm not a coward anymore.

I move toward the door of the diner because I'm not going down without a fight. I love Maren. I know she loves me.

I feel it.

Whoever the man is that she's clinging to, he needs to get in line behind me, because I already gave my heart to Maren, and I don't want it back.

Just as I'm about to reach for the door handle, my phone rings.

I curse under my breath even though no one around me will fine me for swearing.

I tug my phone out of my pocket.

Earl Newman's name lights up the screen of my phone.

I silence it because he needs to wait.

I hold the door open for a woman with a stroller. She struggles to maneuver the wheels through the narrow entryway, so I help out. I take over the handle and guide it through all while the small brown-haired baby inside keeps napping.

"Thank you." She turns to me. "Most men in this city wouldn't help my son and me out."

"Most men in this city are assholes," I quip.

She drops her gaze to the diamond ring nestled next to a wedding band on her hand. "My husband, Griffin, doesn't qualify. You don't either. I hope Ellis grows up to be a gentleman too."

"It sounds like he has a great role model in your

husband." I look down at the little boy. "Cute name, by the way."

"It's my maiden name." She smiles. "I won't keep you, but thank you again."

I force a smile as she makes her way toward an empty table.

The ringing of my phone drops my gaze down to the screen again.

I answer as I watch Maren walk toward the washroom leaving the guy in the gray suit alone.

"Earl," I say his name. "How are you?"

His answer sets me back a step. I fumble to grab hold of the wall, but I'm left grasping at air.

As I stumble out of the diner and onto the sun-soaked sidewalk, my world goes dark.

"I'll be there," I tell him solemnly. "I'm on my way."

———

FOUR HOURS LATER, I feel like I've been in the ring with a prizefighter.

I'm sitting at a bar on Madison Avenue, relying on my common sense to dictate how much alcohol I'll pour down my throat tonight.

So far, the scotch is winning.

I'm on my third.

I lost everything in a matter of a few hours.

Maren met up with some chump in a cheap suit at a diner.

Before that, she apparently had coffee with her friends while she was sitting at a table next to a friend of Patrika Newman.

Millions of people call Manhattan home, but the degrees of separation are minuscule.

Earl let me have it. He won't work with a liar, he said.

I don't blame him.

Finn Remsen will be celebrating tonight.

I glance at my phone when it starts to ring again.

Maren might think the third times the charm, but I silence it the same way I did the last two times she's called.

I haven't read any of her text messages either because what the fuck am I supposed to say?

*Who is the guy in the suit you met up with today?*

She sent me a text ten minutes before I spotted her at the diner.

I don't need to reread that text message. I saved it to heart.

**Maren:** *I'll be on my way soon. I can't wait for tonight. It feels like the start of something amazing for us.*

*Us.*

I hate that fucking word.

I finish what's left in my glass and tap the top of the bar to gain the server's attention.

She walks toward me with a grin on her face. "Do you want another?"

I nod.

"I'm Kendall." She leans an elbow on the bar. "What's your name?"

She's pretty. At one point in the past, I would have already asked her to meet up with me after her shift.

The problem is that she's not Maren.

I push back from the bar. "I changed my mind."

Tugging a few bills from the front pocket of my jeans, I toss them on the bar.

"Thanks," she says brightly. "I hope to see you again soon."

She won't.

I'm not traveling down that same fucked-up path I did before. I'm going home to bed. I'll sleep this off, and tomorrow I'll figure out what comes next.

Stepping onto the sidewalk outside the bar, I'm met with a gust of wind.

My phone vibrates in my pocket. I need to look at the fucking thing if I'm going to get an Uber, so I tug it out.

A text message from Maren greets me.

**Maren:** *I'm scared. Please tell me you're okay. Please, Keats.*

I type back a response. It's all I can manage because the screen is so fucking blurry.

**Keats:** *I need time.*

I press send, order an Uber, and silence my phone.

# CHAPTER FIFTY-FIVE

***MAREN***

"THIS ISN'T the same as what happened with Kollin." Bianca reaches for my hand. "It's not, Maren."

When she texted me this morning to find out how dinner went last night, I sent her a simple reply: I need you.

She rushed over here.

She didn't time her arrival, but it happened minutes after Arietta left to take Dudley to doggy daycare on her way to work.

Arietta is the one who sat by my side last night. She could tell something was wrong when I was sitting on the couch in my sweatpants crying when she got home from work.

I have no idea what went so wrong.

When I got to Keats's townhouse after meeting with Royce, he wasn't home.

I banged on the door to try and rouse him because I thought he might have drifted off.

Neither of us has gotten much sleep recently.

When he didn't answer, I called him.

I left a message and then another.

I finally left the steps of his townhouse with one last look at the locked door.

On my way home, the caterer I had hired called to confirm that the event was canceled.

Athena sent me a text thanking Keats and me for donating the bouquet to one of the nursing homes in the city. She noted that she was breaking it up into smaller bouquets so everyone would have a bit of sunshine to brighten their day.

Keats canceled our dinner with the Newmans without a word to me.

Arietta assured me that it was likely because Fletcher chose Finn over him.

That might be true, but why would Keats not tell me that? Why is he still avoiding me?

I glance down at the only text he sent to me.

**Keats:** *I need time.*

I turn my phone's screen to show Bianca the text message.

Her eyes close. "Fuck."

My eyes tear. "It's the same."

"No," she insists. "This is not the same."

It's close enough.

"I need to go away."

My instinct to hide from the world kicked in almost immediately. I've learned that pain follows you everywhere you go, but it's easier to deal with when you're not in the same city as the person who broke your heart.

"I'll go with you," she offers. "I can rent a car. I remember how to get there."

Bianca put her life on hold to go to the Adirondack Mountains with me just days after Kollin dumped me. We stayed at my parents' remote cabin near Tupper Lake. We hiked, we fished, we swam in the water, and I healed.

"I want to go alone."

Her head shakes. "I don't think that's a good idea, Maren. If you want my advice, I think you should talk to Keats first. How do you know this isn't how he processes losing a potential client? Maybe he's sulking."

*Maybe he's a cold-hearted jerk.*

"I need to go away." I shake my head. "I have a lot to think about."

She knows that I met with Royce, but I didn't tell her that he offered me the opportunity of a lifetime. It reaches beyond the promotion I wanted.

I explained to him that I needed to talk to my boyfriend because the decision would impact both of us.

*Us.*

There is no us.

She moves closer. She tugs locks of my hair out from under the neckline of the hoodie I'm wearing. "Promise me you'll be careful. Don't swim alone, and when you go to town, you'll call me?"

I nod.

"I'll help you pack."

I turn to her. "Dudley needs to go back to Keats. I don't think Arietta will give him up."

She wraps her arm around my shoulder. "I'll take care of it. I'll take of it all."

I know she will. She did the last time I was left with nothing but empty words and a broken heart.

---

CHARMING IS the word my dad uses to describe our family cabin. My mom's positive spin on it is that it's quaint.

I love it because it's remote.

The cabin consists of six-hundred feet of cramped space, including one bedroom, a bathroom, a small kitchen, and three plastic chairs next to a round table.

There's no television here. WiFi and cell service don't exist in this part of the state.

This is the place my parents always brought me when they needed an escape from the demands of New York City.

I drop my bag and the keys from the rental car on the table.

I look around at the dusty interior of the cabin.

Pressing the light switch, I gaze up at the strings of small white lights my dad hung up years ago. It was magical to me then, and it still is.

This place is nothing like my apartment in Manhattan, but I love it here. I need to be here.

I drop onto the old blue and green checkered sofa that doubles as a pullout bed.

Circling my arms around my chest, I sob.

I cry for what I've lost in the past and for what I've lost now.

I thought I had a chance at real happiness, but maybe that's not how my story is supposed to end.

# CHAPTER FIFTY-SIX

***Keats***

SCRUBBING my hand over the back of my neck, I glance outside my townhouse for the fiftieth fucking time.

"The goddamn package isn't here," I say to the guy I'm talking to. "If you delivered it, it's fucking invisible."

"Oh, no, Keats," a quiet voice says.

*Shit.*

I turn to see Stevie standing ten feet away from me.

I shake my head, trying to mouth an apology to her. I'm losing it. I am fucking losing it because I miss Maren.

"Maybe someone snatched it off your porch, sir," he says into my ear. "Did you ever think of that?"

I peer out the window to look at my stoop again. "I didn't."

"If you have surveillance equipment, I suggest you check that before you call back again."

He hangs up.

I don't blame him. I was a dick. I admit it.

I shove the phone into the back pocket of my jeans.

"You swore," Stevie points out. "What's wrong, Keats?"

Berk wanders into the room. He knows the story. I laid it all out last night for him after Stevie went to bed.

He told me to stop punishing Maren for Amber's misdeeds.

Then he scolded me for putting so much pressure on myself to land a deal with Fletcher.

I needed the lecture.

It's been a long time coming.

When you're cheated on, you question your worth. I know that. I felt it.

I tied mine to my work, so whenever I'd lose a potential client, it hit hard.

That's what happened when Earl Newman told me I was the wrong man for the job.

He was right.

I am the wrong man.

I've taken on too much to prove a point to no one but myself.

My life needs an overhaul beginning with my relationship with Maren.

I've tried texting her twice today. My call to her went straight to voicemail, and she hasn't been at work in two days.

I want to talk to her. Even if she breaks my heart, I need to know what she wants and who she wants.

"Did you find out where the package is, Keats?" Stevie asks.

I drag myself back into this moment in time. My niece is looking for the new sneakers I ordered for her. Who the fuck knew that a kid's feet could outgrow a pair of shoes in a month?

"He said the package was delivered. I need to check the doorbell camera footage to see if someone took it."

Stevie gasps as she clings to Budley. "Someone stole my shoes? Call the police, Daddy."

Berk chuckles. "Let's try and solve this mystery ourselves first."

She bounces up and down. "I am a super good detective. I always find your phone when you hide it."

I nod my head in agreement. "She has a valid point."

Stevie taps her fingers on my wrist. "Look at the doorbell camera so we can see who the bad guy is."

My money is on Mrs. Comtors. I caught her red-handed when she tried to lift the flowerpot that used to sit on my stoop.

I carried it the two blocks to her place and warned her to keep her hands off my stuff.

She winked and told me if she were thirty years younger, my stuff would be happy to have her hands on it.

I open the doorbell app and scroll through the dated footage. The delivery information puts the package on my stoop the afternoon that the Newmans were supposed to come for dinner.

I start the video at the time I left to walk to a bodega three blocks from here. I passed that fucking diner where I saw Maren and the blond guy.

I fast forward through it quickly, only picking up shots of people strolling past my townhouse.

I slow it when a white delivery van stops.

Stevie yanks on my forearm. "I want to see it too. Please, Keats."

I drop to one knee and hold the phone between us. "That's when the sneakers were delivered."

She leans closer to the screen. "My shoes. I see the box."

We watch as a delivery guy rings the bell. He says something, but I don't have the voice feature activated during recordings, so I read his lips.

*"Where are you, Mr. Morgan? Answer the damn door, so I can get something to eat."*

I shake my head.

He takes another deep breath before he drops the box at his feet and leaves.

"He just left them there." Stevie shrugs. "He didn't care."

Berk walks up behind us. "He did his job. It's not his fault if someone took them."

I fast forward through the footage again. A few dogs walk by with their owners. I have to stop so Stevie can admire them.

When I spot a flash of red hair in the corner of the frame, my heart stalls in my chest.

"That's Maren!" Stevie screams. "I see Maren."

So do I.

I check the timestamp. It's less than an hour after I saw her at the diner.

I was with Earl Newman then being chastised for lying to his family about my relationship with Maren.

I didn't tell him that I fell in love with her.

Maren approaches my stoop dressed in jeans and a white sweater. The low-heeled boots on her feet are worn on the toes. Her hair is blowing in the light breeze.

She looks just as she did at the diner.

The three of us watch in silence as she knocks on the door twice. Her finger reaches out to ring the bell, and then again.

Her brow furrows as she yanks her phone out of her bag.

I watch her fingers move over the screen.

She's trying to call me. The timestamp on the video matches the missed call on my phone. The voicemail she left was quick and to the point. "I'm standing on your stoop. Open the door."

She tilts her head. Her lips move, and I lean closer to the screen.

"*Where are you?*"

Her finger jabs the doorbell again.

She tries to call again. When I listened to the second voicemail message yesterday, I heard the slight panic in her voice, and I see it on her face now. "Keats, I need to prepare for the party. The caterers are coming soon. Let me in."

"Maren wants to see you, I think." Stevie elbows me.

I don't respond. I'm riveted to the screen watching every move Maren makes.

She finally takes a step back, glances up at the front of the house, and then looks directly at the door.

"*Please, be okay, Keats. I love you.*"

The phone tumbles from my shaking hands.

Berk's hand lands on my shoulder. "I saw it too. I read her lips."

"What did she say?" Stevie's gaze volleys between her dad and me.

"She said she loved me." I don't recognize my voice.

Stevie drops Budley so she can cradle my face in her small hands. "You love her too, don't you?"

Tears prick at the corners of my eyes. "I do."

"I want to be a flower girl at your wedding." She smiles. "I promise I'll do my best, Keats."

"I promise to do my best too." I kiss her forehead. "I'm going to do everything I can to get Maren back."

# CHAPTER FIFTY-SEVEN

***K**EATS*

ARIETTA, Maren's roommate, is a goddamn ghost.

I swear to fuck I can never catch her at home. Or she's actively avoiding me because she wants to keep Dudley forever.

I'm leaning toward the second explanation since Maren told me that Arietta loves that dog.

Ricky raises a hand in the air to me.

It's the fifth time he's done that since I sat down on this bench twenty minutes ago. Tonight, Arietta isn't going to win this silent battle we're in the middle of.

I'm staying put until she gets home from work or takes Dudley for a walk before bed.

Ricky scurries across the marble floor toward the door of the building.

I lined his palm with a hundred dollar bill with the hope that he'd tell me if Arietta is already upstairs.

After he pocketed the cash, he explained that he lives by the rule of conscience.

I asked what the fuck that was. He laughed and said it meant that he couldn't sell out the residents of the building.

I would have saved myself some money if I knew that sooner.

He opens the door and smiles.

In walks a brunette that I recognize immediately.

Maybe my luck is changing for the better.

I bolt to my feet and sprint toward her. She stops as soon as she notices me on the approach.

"Bianca," I call out.

Her blue eyes narrow. "What are you doing here?"

Isn't it obvious? I'm here to find Maren.

"I need to see Maren." I take a step to the left to try and lure her away from Ricky.

I don't need the doorman in my business. He's not my friend. He's not even my informant. He's a guy who stole a hundred dollars from me.

"You hurt her," she accuses.

I nod. "I did. I'm so fucking sorry for that."

"You should be sorry. You need to apologize to Maren, not me."

She's right. I want to do that. "I can't find her."

Her gaze hits the floor. She leans back on her heels. "Do you care about her, Keats?"

"I love her," I say with conviction. "I am so fucking crazy about her."

Her gaze darts to the elevator. "Let's go somewhere to talk. I came to get the dog from Arietta to bring him to you, but that can wait."

Everything can wait until I have Maren back in my arms.

NEVER UNDERESTIMATE the power of your words.

It's a mistake I've made countless times in the past. I did it again with Maren.

Bianca told me everything hours ago as we sat at a café facing each other.

Maren went to meet her boss the afternoon Earl Newman told me to go to hell.

That was Royce Knott she was hugging. He took off because his longtime girlfriend had dumped him, and while he was gone, his brother fired Maren.

That embrace was innocent. It was Maren being compassionate because that's who she is.

Even after everything she's been through.

I glance out the window of the car into the darkness. I called up the driver I've used on occasion and offered him a ridiculous amount of money to make the five-hour drive to take me to Tupper Lake. Bianca drew me a map to the location of the cabin where Maren is staying.

She did it from memory because she was here with her once.

It was days after Maren lost her baby. She was bleeding when her boyfriend, Kollin, took her to the hospital. When the doctor came in to tell them that the child growing inside of Maren for twenty-two weeks had died, Kollin rushed out of the examining room.

An hour later, he sent a three-word text to Maren: I need time.

He never spoke to her again. He packed up her belongings that afternoon and had them sent to her parents' apartment. He arranged for the manager of Human Resources to fire her hours later under the guise that they were cutting costs.

She didn't give him the son they were expecting, so he pushed her out of his life with a short text message.

"How much longer?" I ask the driver, my impatience seeping into my tone.

"We're five minutes out, Mr. Morgan."

Just five more minutes until I can tell Maren I love her.

I rest my head back on the seat, close my eyes, and hope to hell she'll forgive me.

# CHAPTER FIFTY-EIGHT

*MAREN*

I FELL asleep after a late dinner.

I made myself a meal that consisted of scrambled eggs and fruit. I stopped to buy supplies at a store in Tupper Lake before I drove up to the cabin. The couple that runs the store recognized me from the visits I used to make with my parents.

A sense of nostalgia rushed through me as they talked about how happy we always looked on our way to our retreats.

I've always viewed my time here like that - a retreat.

It's an escape from the stress of New York City and a chance to recharge and revaluate my life.

Sitting up in the bed, I hear the crunching sound of gravel.

That can only signal that a vehicle is making its way down the road that leads here and to a few other cabins.

I glance at the digital alarm clock on the bedside table.

It's almost three a.m., so I've been asleep for more than four hours.

I swing my feet over the side of the bed. I let out a short, quick breath when I feel the coolness of the old wood floors on my toes.

Wrapping one of the thin white blankets on the bed around myself, I stand.

I didn't consider how cold the nights get at this time of year when I was packing. I should have brought something warmer than a pair of yoga shorts and a T-shirt to sleep in.

I take a step toward the kitchen to get a glass of water when I hear a light tap on the front door. It's the only door in and out of the cabin.

Fear grips me from the inside out.

I move fast, grasping in the dark for the baseball bat that my dad always kept hidden next to the bed.

He never needed it. The only people who stopped at the cabin were the neighbors. Their visits usually involved a campfire by the lake and cookies with mugs filled with hot chocolate or apple cider.

Another knock fills the silence.

I walk on shaking legs to the doorway of the bedroom. That gives me a clear line of sight to the door of the cabin, but it's solid wood so I can't see who is standing on the other side.

I inch closer, holding the bat in the air.

Another knock greets me.

I could pretend I'm not here, but that won't scare away a would-be intruder, so I call out, "Who is it?"

"It's me."

I stumble forward. *Keats is here? How?*

"Maren, please let me in. Please."

I move to the door and turn the rusted lock. When I swing

the door open, I have to blink twice. "You're here? You came all this way?"

He smiles. "I'd go to the ends of the earth for you, Maren. I love you."

---

I STARE at him with the moonlight falling on us. The sky is clear tonight. The air is perfectly crisp.

I took a step toward him when he said those three words.

*Those three words.*

I love you.

Keats loves me.

"Can we go inside?" He glances behind me at the open doorway of the cabin.

I look around. "How did you know where to find me? How did you get here?"

"Bianca," he says her name quietly. "I ran into her in the lobby of your apartment building. She drew me a map, so I got my driver to bring me."

I take that all in. Bianca wouldn't have sent Keats to find me if she didn't believe that it was the right thing to do.

She's always protected me.

"I can drive." Keats chuckles. "But, my hands have been shaking since I saw you tell me that you love me."

I scrunch my brow. "What?"

"You were on my stoop the day we were supposed to host the Newmans for dinner." He shakes his head. "The day I fucked up."

"You swore," I point out with a slight smile.

He nods. "My doorbell cam recorded you standing there, and I read your lips."

"You read lips?"

His gaze stays on my face. "I do."

I take a chance because isn't that what life's about? Aren't we supposed to dive into the deep end and trust that good things are waiting for us when we surface?

"I love you," I say silently without a sound escaping me.

He leans forward to rest his forehead against mine. "I love you too, Maren. I fucking love you."

# CHAPTER FIFTY-NINE

***Maren***

"I KNOW ABOUT THE BABY, MAREN."

I absorb each of Keats's words one-by-one. I don't look at him. I hold onto the burst of pain that always courses through me when I think about the son I never got to see alive.

Taking a deep breath, I let go and reach for Keats's hand.

He's sitting next to me on the bed. He shed the hoodie he was wearing and his shoes and socks. He's dressed only in jeans now.

His hair is a mess, and I can see something in his eyes I've never noticed before.

Peace, maybe. Or perhaps it's hope.

I feel it too.

"I was going to name him Timmy after my dad."

That was the plan. I hadn't told my dad that before I miscarried. I've never mentioned it since.

We don't discuss that loss.

"That's a beautiful name." Keats reaches for my hand.

"I'm sorry about my text. It was thoughtless. I should have called you that night."

I wrap my fingers around his. "You were upset about losing Fletcher as a client."

Lifting my hand to his lips, he kisses my palm. "I was seething with jealousy because I saw you hugging a man in a diner."

I exhale a breath slowly. "That was Royce."

His eyes lock on mine. "I didn't know that. All I saw was the woman I love more than anything wrapped in another man's arms."

"You thought I was…"

"Cheating?" he finishes my thought. "I thought he was a better man than I am. I was scared that I was losing you."

"I don't cheat," I say clearly. "I wouldn't do that to you. I've never done that to anyone."

Leaning closer, he kisses my cheek. "I should have known that. I let my past dictate my actions. I was rude to you. It was wrong."

I try to piece together everything he's saying.

"So, you saw me with Royce, and then you found out that Fletcher chose Finn over you?"

"Us," he corrects me.

I smile softly. "Us. Do you know why he chose Finn?"

His gaze drops. "It doesn't matter at this point."

It matters to me, so I tell him that. "Tell me."

He gathers both my hands into his lap, holding them firmly in his grasp. "Some friend of Patrika's overheard you talking while you were having a coffee at a café in midtown. You were discussing the fact that the Newmans assumed we were dating, and that got back to Patrika pretty fast."

"Shit." I close my eyes. "I blew it."

Keats lets out a loud chuckle. "You didn't blow it. It happened. It's over."

"You wanted him for a client, Keats."

"I want you, Maren," he counters. "Fletcher was work. This right here is life."

"You're not upset?"

"About losing Fletcher?"

I nod.

"Hell, no." He shakes his head. "Finn will do right by him. He's in good hands."

I move his hands to the center of my chest and hold them there with mine. "I'm in the best hands."

He darts up to his knees. "Damn right, you are."

My gaze falls to the waistband of his jeans and beyond to the outline of his erection beneath the denim. "That'll cost you."

"Name your price." He slides his hands to my shoulders. "I'm not talking money, Maren. Tell me what I owe you."

"Show me how much you love me, Keats."

---

THE CHILL in the air races over my skin, tempering the heat that is blooming there as I near my second orgasm of the night.

I drag my hands through Keats's hair, reveling in how soft the strands are and how rough the scruff on his jaw is as it scrapes against my inner thighs.

I arch my back off the bed when he hones in on my clit with the tip of his tongue.

"Coming," I whisper. "I'm so close to coming."

He hums his approval sending a vibration through my core that lures a deep moan from somewhere inside of me.

"You like that," he whispers.

"So much." I groan.

He applies more pressure. His head moves as he eats me ravenously.

I let go. I close my eyes, and I come with a soul-wrenching cry that brings tears of pure joy to my eyes.

Keats slows his movements. He licks my cleft with long, leisurely strokes of his tongue.

When he looks at me, I see tears in his eyes too.

"I love you, Maren," he whispers as he crawls up my body.

"I love you," I say breathlessly. "I want you."

He rests his forehead against mine. "No condom. I didn't think about bringing any. I just wanted to get to you."

"I'm clean," I offer.

His eyes search mine. "I'm clean too. You're sure you want that?"

The thought of him sliding inside me bare sends a jolt of desire through me. "I want it so much."

He slowly spreads my legs and climbs between them.

With a glance over my body, he lowers his lips to the center of my chest. "You are my life."

I hold my breath as he slides his cock into my channel in one painfully slow movement.

"You are my everything," I whisper. "You will always be."

# EPILOGUE

***One Month Later***

KEATS

"WHY THE FUDGE am I not sneezing around you?" I hold Dudley in the air, so we're face-to-face.

"Dr. Hunt thinks you were allergic to his old shampoo." Arietta stands next to me. "Not him."

I turn to look at her. "I guess this means he can move back in with me."

I watch as her smile drops into a frown. "I don't mind watching him a little longer. Maren said your sister is coming back soon."

Maren is right.

Sinclair is due back in New York next week. I've missed her. My life has completely changed since she's been gone. I can't wait to tell her that I'm in love.

I want to do it in person to see her face when she hears the good news.

"I'm going to drop him off at doggy daycare." She scoops up an oversized black tote. "Tell Maren that I hope she has a good day at work."

I laugh as I take a sip of the coffee I just poured. "She'll be with me, Arietta. How can she not have a hell of a good day?"

"You swore, Keats." She smiles. "You owe a hundred to the fund."

I nod as I watch her walk away. Since Maren and I returned from Tupper Lake a month ago, Arietta and I have spent some time together. We're slowly building a friendship.

"Don't work too hard," I call after her as she nears the door to the apartment she shares with the woman I love.

She turns back to face me. "I wish Mr. Calvetti said those things to me."

"You wish he said a lot of other things to you." Maren comes out of her bedroom dressed for the day.

I left her tangled in the sheets after I woke her with my head between her legs. We finished off with her on top of me, sliding her body over mine as we both whispered how grateful we are to wake up this way every fucking day.

We haven't spent a night apart since we got back from the cabin. We've spent a few nights here and the rest at my townhouse.

*Our townhouse.*

Maren has already started packing so she can move in with me.

Arietta's gaze drops to the floor. "I don't wish for that."

"Is there another office romance blooming?" I wash that question down with a mouthful of coffee.

Arietta shifts her attention back to me. Her cheeks are rosy. A smile is luring the corners of her lips up. "I'm going to start using a dating app soon, so the answer to that is a big no."

With that, she opens the door and walks out, leaving me alone with the most beautiful redhead in the world.

---

AN HOUR LATER, we're at the office.

Maren decided to continue working with me even though Royce Knott offered her the opportunity to buy out his brother's shares to become a partner in what would have been Knott & Weber Public Relations.

She thought long and hard about it. We talked it through, but ultimately the decision was hers to make.

Her future is next to me. We both know that. She wants to help me handle the client list I have, and together, we will selectively choose athletes to pursue in the future.

Maren has her eye on a tennis ace. She's nineteen, new to the circuit, and incredibly talented.

My love wants to take the lead on this one, so I'm all for that. Morgan Sports Management is going to take on a new partner in the form of my future wife.

I watch as she sits behind my desk, typing something on my laptop.

"You're beautiful," I whisper.

She glances up to where I'm standing next to the window. "You're handsome as fuck."

I bite back a smile. "You swore."

"I owe a hundred." She sighs. "I pinkie swore with Stevie. I need to pay up just like the rest of the family."

*The family.*

That's exactly what we are.

"I'm sending an email to Fletcher Newman," she announces. "You're not going to believe what's going on with him."

I hope it's all good news. He's a great young man with a future that is overflowing with possibility.

Turning to face her, I lift my chin. "Tell me."

"He didn't sign with Finn after all." She leans back in her chair. "He's going back to school to study architecture."

I shake my head, unsure if I heard her correctly. "What?"

"He wrote to me and said that he realized that he loves to watch baseball, but playing is not his passion."

The sport lost a promising talent, but the world gained someone willing to chase their dreams. That's a win in my book.

"I'm setting up a meeting between him and Myles Sims. He's the best architect in this city. Maybe he can mentor Fletcher."

I don't need to ask who Myles is to her because I know he's not the guy who holds her heart in his hands. I'm that lucky bastard.

"Myles is another cousin of mine." She laughs. "I have a lot of them all over this city."

She taps her finger over the keyboard before she pushes back to stand.

"Remember the day I walked in and found you covered in glitter with a champagne bottle in your hand?"

I huff out a laugh. "How the heck could I forget that?"

"That's how I want you on our wedding night." She smiles. "Carefree, happy, and without pants."

I don't hear any of that but the wedding night part. "Are you asking me to marry you?"

Her beautiful blue eyes slide over my face. "You've asked me twice in the past twenty-four hours."

She's right. I have. Both times happened when we were in her bed.

I drop to a knee to do it right this time. Reaching into the inside pocket of my suit jacket, I pull out a small square box.

Maren's hand darts to her mouth. "You have a ring?"

I bought it the day we came back from Tupper Lake because I knew she was my every tomorrow. I went to Whispers of Grace. It's a jewelry store run by Ivy Marlow-Walker. She's gifted when it comes to creating timeless pieces. I chose a silver band with one stunning ruby in the center and a circle of small diamonds surrounding it.

I pop open the lid.

Maren lets out a gasp. "Keats."

"I didn't plan on doing this in our office, but what the he…heart. It's about our hearts, so it doesn't matter where it happens."

She nods. "You're right."

"I'm indebted to you for showing me that love can be this good. For accepting me and all my faults and for giving me a chance to believe that the future can be amazing." I take a breath as I stare up and into her eyes. "I love you more than Stevie loves unicorns or seals, or whatever she'll love next. Marry me, Maren. I'll make every day we have together better than the last."

Her head bobs up and down as tears fill her eyes. "I'll marry you. Of course, I'll marry you."

I slide the ring on her finger, jump to my feet, and take her in my arms.

"Our adventure has only started," she tells me before she kisses me.

She's damn right. The very best is yet to come.

*Do you want to see what happens next for Maren and Keats? Click here.*

## ALSO BY DEBORAH BLADON
### & SUGGESTED READING ORDER

The Obsessed Series

The Exposed Series

The Pulse Series

Impulse

The Vain Series

Solo

The Ruin Series

The Gone Series

Fuse

The Trace Series

Chance

The Ember Series

The Rise Series

Haze

Shiver

Torn

The Heat Series

Risk

Melt

The Tense Duet

Sweat

Troublemaker

Worth

Hush

Bare

Wish

Sin

Lace

Thirst

Compass

Versus

Ruthless

Bloom

Rush

Catch

Frostbite

Xoxo

He Loves Me Not

Bittersweet

## THANK YOU

Thank you for purchasing and downloading my book. I can't even begin to put to words what it means to me. If you enjoyed it, please remember to write a review for it. Let me know your thoughts! I want to keep my readers happy.

For more information on new series and standalones, please visit my website, www.deborahbladon.com. There are book trailers and other goodies to check out.

If you want to chat with me personally, please LIKE my page on Facebook. I love connecting with all of my readers because without you, none of this would be possible. www.facebook.com/authordeborahbladon

Thank you, for everything.

## ABOUT THE AUTHOR

Deborah Bladon has never read a romance hero she didn't like. Her love for romance novels began when she was old enough to board the bus, library card in hand to check out the newest Harlequin paperbacks. She's a Canadian by heart, and by passport, but you can often spot her in New York City sipping a latte and looking for inspiration for her next story. Manhattan is definitely her second home.

She cherishes her family and believes that each day is a gift for writing, for reading, and for loving.

Printed in Great Britain
by Amazon